**"I know w...
through your mind."**

Pagan watched her. "You don't trust me to be the perfect gentleman," he said. "Well, I never was a man to bow to convention...."

"Maybe that's why people said you and Roxanne were made for each other," Jane responded. "You both break rules."

"Yes, but I would never harm the innocent. I can see the innocence in your eyes. They're elusive, changing like the sea as it tosses at the rocks and fights to batter them down. It takes many turns of tide to finally wear down a rock to sand grains."

"So I'm the water and you're the rock, is that it?" Jane asked incredulously.

"Isn't it?"

But she couldn't answer. No one gentle as herself could hope to influence a man as strong—and as tragic—as Pagan Pentrevah.

VIOLET WINSPEAR
is also the author of these

Harlequin Presents

and these

Harlequin Romances

Many of these titles are available at your local bookseller.

For a free catalogue listing all available Harlequin Romances and Harlequin Presents, send your name and address to:

HARLEQUIN READER SERVICE,
M.P.O. Box 707, Niagara Falls, NY 14302
Canadian address: Stratford, Ontario N5A 6W2

VIOLET WINSPEAR

a girl possessed

Harlequin Books

TORONTO • LONDON • LOS ANGELES • AMSTERDAM
SYDNEY • HAMBURG • PARIS • STOCKHOLM • ATHENS • TOKYO

Harlequin Presents edition published March 1981
ISBN 0-373-10420-0

Original hardcover edition published in 1980
by Mills & Boon Limited

CHAPTER ONE

JANIE SPUN THE WHEEL and the car rounded the bend smoothly enough. Then joltingly the nearside wheel hit an object and the next instant she was struggling not to skid over the cliff as the tire blew out.

With her heart thudding under her ribs Janie sat there and could hardly believe that she and the vehicle hadn't pitched over the edge of the narrow road and gone bouncing and breaking down on the rocks where the intense blue sea beat at them, sending up shafts of glittering water.

"Janie, that was a close one!" she chastened herself, leaning on the steering wheel and catching her breath. Across the sea a swath of red was spreading, a warning that the sun was setting and night was coming. She gazed at the scenery, a vivid fresco of blue, green and flame, and felt glad to be alive. A minor miracle considering how close that torn tire had hurtled her car to the edge of the road, leaving her stranded in the beautiful middle of nowhere.

She was in the heart of Cornwall, somewhere on the road to St. Mawgan, and that was all she knew. On leaving the café where she had lunched she had stupidly left her map lying on the table, and for the past few hours she had been driving by guesswork. Jane Larue was on her way to a job, that of driver and companion to a Mrs. Burford, a friend of her grandmother's. Janie was an out-of-work actress but like all human beings she needed to eat and keep reasonably covered in clothing, so at Grandma Polly's urging she had agreed to take this job until a stage offer came along.

"Things were so much better for actresses in my day," Grandma Polly had remarked. "People went more often to the theater and they paid reasonable prices for a seat. Be a sensible girl, Janie, get yourself a nice young man and let him keep you—in holy wedlock, of course!"

"Of course," Janie had laughed. "It wouldn't do for me to be a thoroughly Modern Jane, would it?"

"Love the man and he'll love you in return," her grandmother advised with the conviction of a past generation.

"I think love's an illusion," was Janie's rejoinder. "It's a lovely fiction that has little to do with real life." She wanted beyond anything to act in exciting plays but so far her dream was unrealized. She remained convinced that she could act but it seemed that her star was not yet ready to sprinkle her with its magic dust.

A bit of a dreamer, Grandma Polly was inclined to call her, and Janie was the first to agree that she preferred romance to reality. Even her present predicament couldn't spoil the awe and enchantment she felt as the sun slid down the sky and cast its brazen glow across the surface of the Atlantic Ocean. Her gaze lifted to the sky and her green gray eyes were entranced by the array of colors spilling out around the dying sun.

"Gorgeous!" she murmured, and in her imagination she heard a peal of Wagner music echoing over the water. It was Janie's blessing as well as her burden that she dramatized everything that touched her life.

It had kept her curiously innocent at the age of twenty-two, and in a milieu where affairs of the heart were a common occurrence it had kept her chaste. When Jane Larue looked at a man with her wide-set eyes he felt as he might have done in the presence of a novice, and the Joan of Arc way she wore her hair added to her untouched look. The part of Joan was one that Janie longed to play and in dreamy expectation of this miracle her hair was smoothly bobbed and fringed above eyes that gleamed gray green when her mood was somber; green gray when her spirits took flight.

She glanced around her and saw dusky shadows stealing across the countryside. Soon it would be dark and there was little sense in sitting here in a car that was out of action. She hadn't a spare tire and when she climbed from her seat and took a look at the damaged one it was plain that she hadn't a hope of driving any farther with a wheel so badly ripped. She'd have to abandon the sports car and seek shelter for the night. There had to be houses somewhere in the vicinity and having been brought up in the country Janie knew that countryfolk were inclined to be more hospitable than townspeople.

The sun went down and for a few brief moments the afterglow was vivid. Then it faded and the dusk slid its soft and scented mantle over the cliffs, the sea and the moors.

Janie reached into the car for her suede jacket and the smaller of her two suitcases.

She wasn't unnerved by the approach of night; as a girl born and bred in the country she knew there was more safety in fields than in city streets.

Luckily she had a small flashlight in the car and for at least twenty-five minutes she followed the thin beam of light along the winding road. Birds going to roost called to one another as they swooped around the looming cliffs; far below Janie could hear the tide swishing in over the stony sands and the rocks. The tang of the sea was in her nostrils and the air had freshened to the point of chilliness. She pulled the collar of her jacket up around her neck and felt a grumbling inside her that reminded her that lunch had been a long time ago. Gosh, how she would have welcomed a cup of hot tea and several cheese sandwiches spread with plowman's relish.

Was that a light?

She stood still and gazed across the rambling stone wall beside which she had been walking for some time. Again the light winked at her through foliage, possibly a group of trees in a grove. On impulse she climbed over the wall, tossing her suitcase ahead of her, and though aware that Cornwall was bog country in parts began to cross the moor, beckoned by that glimmer in the darkness.

Dew spattered the backs of her legs, for the grass was knee-high, and eerie little sounds echoed back and forth as she invaded the territory of night creatures.

Overhead the sky had become littered with stars, and without being nervous Janie was aware of being a stranger in a strange land where a lot of time had stood still. The gothic land of Arthur where the knights of the round table had sworn to fight for glory and the grail. Merlin's country where he had cast his spells and runes, and where the tall stones stood in memory of mystic rites carried out by moonlight.

Suddenly Janie's flashlight started to flicker a warning that the battery was running out and even as she felt a stab of dismay the wind across the moor lifted the bough of a tree and she saw clearly the outline of a window—a long oval window glowing amber in the night.

"Thank heaven!" she breathed, and plowed on through the grass toward the beckoning light.

Blessed light that promised shelter, a cup of steaming tea, and hopefully a telephone so she could let Mrs. Burford know that she'd had trouble with her car and wouldn't arrive at St. Mawgan until some time tomorrow.

A light glowing in the night can seem close and yet be some distance away and Janie hadn't tramped across a moor for some years, having been busy learning the craft of acting and getting bit parts in plays. She could feel a muscle pulling in the calf of her leg and was growing weary of shifting her case from one hand to the other in order to ease the burden. And now that her flashlight was failing she had grown increasingly aware of the solitary old trees standing around on the moor, bent and gnarled, like witches in waiting.

A nursery jingle wandered into her mind and wouldn't go away. "Bogey Bogey, don't catch me! Catch the girl in the apple tree!"

Abruptly she became aware of a sound that was unrelated to a bird or a rabbit darting through the grass. Her heart hammered and she turned startled as the sound thudded out of the darkness and was suddenly fearfully upon her.

"Whoa, boy!" The large horse reared up, pawing the air with its forelegs, so close that Janie felt a gust of heat from the animal's body.

"Devil take it—" The rider stared down at her, his brows as black as the windblown hair across his broad forehead. Why she saw him so vividly was due to a final flicker of life from her flashlight, which lighted

the man's face for half an instant then left him in
darkness through which his eyes still seemed to glimmer.

"What are you doing scaring my mount?" he demanded.

"Y-you scared me," she gasped, "half to death!"

"What the deuce are you doing on the moor at this
time of night? Are you lost, girl?"

"Yes. I'm heading for that house." She gestured in
the direction of the lighted window, wishing fervently
that the house and its occupants were nearer.

"That's my house," he said curtly. "Pentrevah
Towers."

"Yours?" Again she felt a shock of alarm and dismay.

"Settle down, Salem." His hand must have tightened on the rein for the animal snorted and tossed its
head making the bridle jingle. "I'm Pagan Pentrevah
and you are on my land, young woman. I own this
stretch of moorland and the house beyond it."

"Pagan?" Janie had never heard anyone called
that, even among theatrical folk who sometimes managed to have rather outlandish names that looked eye-
catching on the theater marquee.

"I collected the name at my christening so it isn't
something I've invented." There was in the man's
voice a sound Janie hadn't heard before and she realized that it had to be the sound of someone Cornish
who had been well educated and was a gentleman
rather than a farmer. It was a deep voice with smoldering undertones, matching well the black brows that
slanted above eyes that had struck her as unusual even
in that brief glimpse she had of them. Foreign somehow, reminding her that a good deal of Spanish blood
had intermingled with that of the Cornish folk who,

also from way back, had been Celts from across the various seas.

"It suits you." Janie spoke impulsively, and then felt a tide of warmth from her neck to the roots of her hair. It wasn't that she was coy or shy, for working on the stage quickly banished those sort of tendencies. It was the man himself. He emitted vibrations from up there on the black horse; vibrations of mastery and mystery. Janie felt as if her heart was beating too fast and she took a gulp of air.

"So you're heading for the Towers?" he said. "How did you come to be lost on my land, eh?"

"I was driving to St. Mawgan when my car got a flat tire. I couldn't just sit there so I decided to try and find shelter for the night. I-I saw a light in that window so I headed for it."

"I don't know whether to say that was wise of you or foolish." A low, brief laugh issued from him. "Are you afraid of horses?"

"Not in the least," she asserted. "I was brought up in the country; my grandfather had a farm and I lived there until I was eighteen."

"When you went off to seek fame and fortune, eh?"

"How did you guess?"

"This is Merlin the Wizard's land, surely you know that much?"

"Yes, but—"

"Just a superstition you're thinking, miss?"

"Isn't it, Mr. Pentrevah?"

"Not entirely. What takes you to St. Mawgan?"

"I have a job waiting there for me."

"Let it wait," he said decisively. "Now give me your hand and step on my boot and I'll hoist you up here on the saddle."

"I have a suitcase with me...." She stood there hesitantly, quite unafraid of the horse but distinctly wary of the rider. In the fading beam of her flashlight she had seen the strength in his features and in the shoulders clothed by a black sweater with the collar to his chin. That hair of his had looked sable, the hue of worn armor. He gave her the feeling that he could be more ruthless than kind.

"Bogey, Bogey, don't catch me!" The jingle flickered through her mind again.

"Scared of me?" he gibed. "Afraid you've crossed the footpath of the Devil, as we say in these parts?"

"H-how do I know you are who you say you are?" she said defensively.

"My credit cards are in my other coat," he rejoined. "If you want to walk the rest of the way to the Towers, then do so, but Salem will get you there a lot sooner and I imagine you're gasping for a cup of tea."

"I'm dying for one, but what about my suitcase?"

"Throw it in a bush and you can collect in the morning. Salem is somewhat tempered and he wouldn't take kindly to the thing banging on his back."

She saw the reason in his reply but all the same the case had her night things in it as well as her toiletries. If she was going to spend the night at the Towers....

"Do you usually take this long to come to a decision?" he inquired.

"The case has my requirements in it."

"Don't let that bother you. My house is a well-stocked one and I'm sure Agatha can supply you with whatever you need."

Agatha? Janie breathed a quiet sigh of relief and did as she was told with regard to the suitcase. She then extended a hand to Pagan Pentrevah, who was mar-

ried after all, and felt the strong grip of fingers cal-
loused from handling a mettlesome horse.

"That's it, up with you." Salem did a side dance as
she mounted, then a muscular arm was holding her
securely to a broad chest. The next instant they were
galloping across the moor and Janie knew that the
Bogey Man had caught her...as somehow the moor
had warned her from the moment she had climbed
that drystone wall to follow the light beckoning to her
from the window of a solitary house.

She felt the vital energy in the man who owned that
house, a strength and endurance possibly drawn from
the wilds of Merlin's land.

"You've suddenly lost your tongue," he remarked.
"Are you thinking you're riding with the devil horse-
man who is said to ride out on the moors on a moon-
less night?"

Since going to London, Janie had been living and
working among people who were ultramodern in their
outlook. This man Pentrevah seemed of another
time, unless it was that his surroundings cloaked him
in their otherworldliness.

"You've rather swept me off my feet, haven't you,
Mr. Pentrevah?"

"That reply could be interpreted two ways, miss.
Which way shall I take it?"

"T-the correct one, if you don't mind!"

Again she felt the breath swept from her throat. It
was such an alarming sensation, one she had only pre-
viously felt when a school chum had swung her too
high in the old swing in the apple orchard at the farm
and she had nearly flown off the seat. She smiled in
memory, and then sobered. Dear Jimmy, he had gone
to be an oil rigger and had died in the cold North Sea

during a terrible gale that had damaged the rig. She shivered and felt the arm of Pagan Pentrevah tighten around her waist.

"Why are London girls always so damned bony? With not much flesh on you, you're bound to feel the cold."

"I told you, Mr. Pentrevah, I'm not really a London girl."

"Then it's been a long time since you sat down to a dish of apple pie with clots of cream. What do you do in London?"

"I...act."

"On the stage?" He sounded amazed, there above her head.

"Yes. I'm an actress." Janie didn't know why she felt on the defensive about the profession she loved, but he seemed the sort who might deride it.

"I wouldn't have taken you for an actress."

"Thanks," she muttered "Do you know many then?"

He didn't answer her right away and she didn't think she imagined the lift of his chest on what might have been a sigh.

"I thought actresses were glamorous," he said bluntly.

"I—I don't play those sort of roles," she said, flushing. "You believe in calling a spade a spade, don't you?"

"I find it's the best way," he agreed. "What are you used to, men who lie their heads off just to get you where they want you?"

"Really!" The flush became a hot trail of fire over her skin, and all at once her body was infinitely aware of the muscular feel of him against her. How arrogant he was! One of those men so sure of himself that he never needed to fabricate lies or manufacture charm in order to get what he wanted from women.

"Don't tell me a girl working in London isn't used to the brave truth?" he mocked. "I thought everyone there was having one hell of a good time; that they were busy turning the town into a modern Babylon."

"Parts of it are getting like that," she had to admit. "Certain sections are very gaudy and gay, but I-I take my craft seriously and that means I don't play around. I haven't the inclination, thank you!"

"Miss Prim and Proper, eh?"

"My name is Jane Larue." She could feel herself putting her nose in the air, a habit she had when a man happened to annoy her.

"Did you say Janet?"

"No, I'm called Janie—by my friends."

"Don't you feel that we're going to be friends?"

"It's hardly likely, is it?" She stiffened as if afraid he was making an overture she wouldn't know how to handle. He was so much bigger than any actor she had worked with, so much more...masculine.

"You never know your luck, Janie." A thread of sardonic humor wove itself into his voice. "A light in my window caught your fancy, didn't it? You'll be sleeping under my roof, won't you?"

Her lips fell apart and her pulse gave a jolt. He made that word sound almost like a threat. Thank goodness for the yet to be met Agatha! Janie swore she would not have entered his house had he been unmarried.

"I'll only be staying the one night," she said distantly. "I hope your wife won't mind putting me up at such short notice?"

"My wife?" He said it in the most curious tone of voice. "What do you know about—my wife?"

"Nothing, Mr. Pentrevah. You just happened to mention that her name was Agatha."

"Agatha is my housekeeper and she's sixty-one years old. Do I look that old?"

"No." Janie was very much shaken by his revelation. "But you certainly look old enough to be married."

"So do you, young woman. Girls hereabouts are married as soon as they can bake a good pie and make a bed so it isn't lumpy. What are you doing, saving yourself for the Great Part?"

"Yes. Acting is all I want." She spoke with feeling. "I don't care if you consider it wonderful for a girl to be a man's cook, cleaner and general drudge. I don't plan to become any man's slave!"

"What if you fall headlong in love? It happens to people whether they want it or not, and women aren't their own mistress when that happens. All they want is to give themselves like faggots to the flames."

"I think love is a myth," Janie rejoined.

As a devotee of Bernard Shaw she was convinced that the great man had been right when he had said that men married for sex and women married for security. It made a lot of sense, that statement from a man who had written such marvelous plays. Maybe if she wasn't an actress but a girl who worked at a factory bench putting lipsticks in boxes, or pickles in jars, then she might see the sense in exchanging the role of factory worker for that of housewife. As it was she was happy to strive for her dream. She saw herself up there on the stage, the audience hushed, the faggots waiting to be fired as she, Joan of Arc, was bound to the stake in sackcloth and ashes.

"I happen to agree with you," said Pagan Pentrevah, "if you're talking about love between the sexes.

But there's another kind of love that comes out of that kind of union—a son or a daughter gets born.''

As he spoke they came to the gates of Pentrevah Towers. Thrusting iron spokes stood atop the gates, which were flung wide to the moor that was all around them as far as the eye could see.

They galloped in under the shifting light of wall lanterns, into a court of flagstones fronting the bulk of the Towers.

Janie gazed wide-eyed at the house with its towering granite walls and a colonnade of pillars supporting the upper regions. Vast, durable, the light from the iron-sconced lanterns flung up against the curved structure of the towers that gave the house its name. High walls roamed all around the place, rugged and protective and overhung with thick foliage.

The light that Janie had glimpsed from across the moor had obviously come from the back of the house; seen from the front it was awesome, not at all the sort of habitation she had set out to find when she had left her car abandoned at the roadside.

"Grip the pommel while I dismount," said the man who had brought her here.

She did as she was told and he slid from the saddle and held his arms in readiness for her to dismount into them. Her feeling of hesitancy and doubt was powerful, a tingling of fear and fascination mixed with it. Never before had Janie met a man as forthright as this one. He was so ruthlessly molded into the shape of a man. Like the cromlechs, she thought, that stood upon the moors, symbols of strange rites and the spelling of the runes.

"Come!" It was a command that stiffened her spine. He was Pentrevah and accustomed to giving orders. Law and land had made him masterful but

Janie felt a disinclination to come to heel at his command.

"I can manage on my own," she said, "if you'll stand back."

"If I stand back, miss, and Salem finds himself alone with a stranger in his saddle, he'll have you out of it and down on those flagstones before you can say Jack Robinson. Now do as you're told!"

"You've a charming way with you!" she flashed.

"Charm is for those with the time to cultivate it, and I don't intend to stand here for an hour while you spit and claw like some silly cat caught up an apple tree. Now swing a leg across Salem's back and I'll catch you. Come, I won't drop you on the ground, if it's that you're afraid of."

She realized that it had to be done. Salem was already fidgeting and it did look a long way to the ground where the stones looked as unyielding as Pagan Pentrevah's face.

She swung a leg, held her breath and dropped into his arms. They caught her without effort and then held her for several taunting moments against the horsey tang of his breeches and black sweater. He gave a brief laugh, which he seemed to hold in his throat. "I thought actresses were the least shy of females," he mocked. "Or is it something about me that makes you tremble like a leaf?"

"I'm doing no such thing—"

"No?" He tightened an arm across her back and deliberately pressed her to him. "I can feel you quaking."

"It's because I-I'm miles from where I ought to be. Women don't like their plans to go wrong."

"That's true," he agreed, very sardonically. "I'll go along with that, Miss Larue. Also you're hungry and gasping for some tea. Do I strike you as a fearful bully?"

"You obviously like your own way, Mr. Pentrevah." She wished fervently that he'd release her from his arms. He was so strong and sure that he made her feel he could do whatever he wished with her, whether she willed it or not. It was this feeling that he could have his will of her that made panic rise in her.

"Please—let me go!" She couldn't contain the plea, no more than she could stop her knees from knocking. The familiarity of London was miles away and she was about to enter a house that looked as if in its time it had held women captive in its stone towers.

"Don't you enjoy the proximity of a man?" he taunted. "Doesn't such a phobia make it a bit awkward for an actress? Or do you act in these modern plays that have nothing to do with normal relationships?"

"I would like to point out that you—you're a stranger to me, Mr. Pentrevah."

"Perhaps men and women are always strangers to one another, even when they live together. Closeness brings no guarantee that you're no longer alone because intimacy has occurred. I'll grant you that, young woman."

His face was hard, as if it would feel like granite, when he made this statement. Janie waited tensely for him to remove his arms from around her body, whose every nerve seemed set on edge by the almost savagely strong closeness of him.

"I think when you get close to people you give them the opportunity to hurt you," she said quietly, suspecting somewhere at the back of her mind that someone had hurt him and he hadn't forgiven it.

"We become vulnerable, eh?"

"Yes."

"You're right, Jane Larue, but who taught you such a cynical truth? Was it a man?"

"Yes," she said again, but didn't add that her tutoring had come from the writings of Shaw, that cynical genius with his pen dipped in a mixture of acid and gold.

A night wind wafted across the court of Pentrevah Towers, brushing Janie's skin and hair, a cold feeling somehow more noticeable because in that moment Pagan Pentrevah let her go.

"You're wanting your supper," he said briskly. "Follow me, Jane, if your knees aren't feeling too weak!"

CHAPTER TWO

JANIE BLINKED HER EYES as she stepped into the hall of Pentrevah Towers. It was another world, one she had never visited before. Her gaze went upward to the timbered vaulting that was dark and smoky with age and hung with large lamps on chains that lighted, at intervals along the hall, unusual paneled cubicles.

"Monk's stalls," she was told. "The stained glass in those windows was brought from across the Tamar, salvaged from a monastery when King Hal decided to dispense with the Jesuits. Magnificent figures, aren't they? That's Apollinaris with the sword and raven, Augustine holding the flaming heart, and there, Blaise carrying the iron combs with which his body was flayed. The Jesuits were always strong on suffering, or don't you know a lot about them?"

Janie shook her head and gazed wonderingly at the range of Gothic windows in which the saints were captured in rich old glass.

"My own favorite is Dominic." He gestured at the figure with a star in his forehead. "There have been Dominics in this family since it was founded and that was a devil of a long time ago."

Janie glanced at him, her attention caught by a somber note in his voice. Under the lamps hanging from the beams his face had a brooding look, with a hint of disillusion lurking around the lines of his mouth.

"The windows are arranged so the saints catch the

sunset," he said. "It's quite a sight, as if they writhe in flames, as some of them certainly did in the cause of faith, hope and charity."

"Souls in torment," she murmured.

"Exactly, but let us hope you never get afflicted by the feeling. It isn't an easy one to live with."

"Do you live with it?" The words escaped her before she could restrain them, and as his face darkened she backed away from him, as if she feared she had been insolent. Something raged in his eyes, and now she saw them clearly, the strange ring of gold around the dense black pupil of each eye, giving to his gaze the menace of a moorland hawk.

"Don't be impertinent," he snapped.

"I-I'm sorry—" She actually shook and felt a weakness in her body, a combination of nerves, hunger and uncertainty. "I didn't mean to sound rude, especially when you've been kind enough to offer me some supper a-and a bed for the night."

"Ah, yes, I'd better see about your comfort." He strode to a cavernous fireplace and tugged at a plaited bell cord that hung there, the old-fashioned type of bellpull that suited the place.

There was a richness of carving, a tang of woodsmoke, a gleam of steel from old weapons affixed to the paneled walls. There was a sense of age, even of antiquity, and yet everything looked cared for and clean, an indication of servants obedient to a rather demanding master.

The tall figure of Pagan Pentrevah stood there against the high stone ledge of the fireplace and despite his breeches and sweater he gave the illusion of being clad in dark armor. A definite illusion Janie knew and yet a significant one. This was a man whose feelings were armored, up to the hilt.

"You blink like a cat that has wandered into a house whose scent and ambience make you wary." He reached to a carved box on the ledge and took from it a thin dark cheroot. He then bent to the fire with a spill and carried the flame to the tip of the cheroot. Janie watched in silent fascination as the flame reflected in his strange eyes. They met hers and one of his black eyebrows raised itself.

"Your eyes are as green as a cat's," he remarked.

"And what do the superstitious Cornish folk say about yours?" This time she did sound pert but wasn't going to apologize for it. She had the distinct feeling that it might be better for her if he flung her out on the moor where sleeping in the heather might be safer than sleeping under his alarming roof.

"There is a story," he said, smoke curling from his lips, "that long ago the wizard Merlin seduced a girl of this family and consequently she had a child with golden eyes. Such eyes as mine have been in the family since the old days. The legend is that every black-haired Pentrevah has the wizard's eyes. Are you afraid I'll cast a spell over you?"

"I'm not a teenager who believes in fairy tales." She said it bravely enough but his gaze did send odd sensations through her body, all the way down to the pit of her stomach.

"Is this your first trip into Cornwall?" he asked.

She nodded. "I'd heard tales about it from my grandmother who has a friend at St. Mawgan with whom she stays now and again. She's the woman I'm going to work for.... Have you a telephone, Mr. Pentrevah? I have to let Mrs. Burford know that I haven't driven off a cliff. She's expecting my arrival today."

"I do have a telephone, but I'd rather like you to postpone your call until later. Do you mind?" His eyes were intent upon Janie through the smoke of his cheroot, something mesmeric about them.

"Would it matter if I minded?" Her hand climbed to the tiny gold horseshoe that hung on a chain against the skin of her throat, her finger pressing the tiny diamond set in the shoe.

"Not a great deal," he casually confessed.

"You're a very arrogant man, aren't you?" She said the words very carefully, in a precise stage voice that carried along the hall to where the stained-glass saints acted out their torments.

"We are, Miss Larue, what fate and fortune make of us. Fate threw a sharp stone where your car would pass over it and as that road is a precarious one you can count yourself lucky you're still in one piece. A motorcyclist came to grief on that road only two weeks ago, though he was probably belting along as if taking part in a race. Were you driving fast?"

"I wasn't speeding."

"But you were in a hurry, eh? The sun was declining and you wanted to get to St. Mawgan before night fell. I take a guess that if you hadn't glimpsed a light in a window of the Towers you'd have kept to the road; it runs through a small village."

Janie caught her breath. The very word village conjured an image of coziness and a welcoming inn where she could have stayed comfortably. It was a word that certainly didn't apply to Pentrevah Towers, which was impressive like its master and gave her a feeling of having stepped out of the modern world into one where the actions of its occupants went unquestioned for the most part.

Her gaze ran the length and breadth of Pagan Pentrevah and again she realized that his type of male was becoming as rare as the tiger.

"Which proves that we all make mistakes and regret them," she said, as provoking him to put her out
into the night.

"There is no doubt," his eyes glinted, "that we all
make mistakes we'd give a hell of a lot to put right."

"Even you, Mr. Pentrevah?"

"Even I, miss."

"How astonishing when you look so big and tough."

"Quite. None of us likes being led astray by jack-
o'-lantern but at least you didn't walk into Prowler's
Pool."

Janie gazed at him inquiringly, but with a sudden
black frown he half turned to the fire so his profile
was hammered out darkly against the smoldering logs.

"Prowler's Pool is a quicksand, and moorland animals such as sheep and ponies have strayed into it
never to be seen again. The bog is on my land.
There's a warning notice up but a girl walking in the
dark wouldn't be likely to see it. You took a chance
when you left the roadside, didn't you?"

"Yes." Janie gave a cold shiver. "It crossed my
mind that there are bogs in Cornwall but we never
think that anything awful is going to happen to our-
selves, do we?"

"Fate lays out the chessboard," he said somberly.
"We're only the pawns in the game. If you had
wandered into the quicksand it would have seemed as
if you had vanished from the face of the earth. As if
like Eurydice you had been whisked off to Hades."

He swung to face her, a flicker of sardonic humor
in his eyes. "Is that how you feel about being here in
my house, as if the lord of the dark regions has you in
his power?"

"I-I refuse to be fanciful," she rejoined. "I'm only
staying the night—I shall be gone in the morning."

In the silence that followed Janie waited for him to agree with her that her stay was limited, but instead he gazed beyond her and spoke to someone who had just entered the hall. "Agatha, will you attend to this young lady and see to it that she has a comfortable bed and some food. We met each other on the moor. Her car had a flat tire."

He returned his attention to Janie. "My housekeeper will see to your wants, Jane. You look a little done in so I suggest you have your supper in bed."

"Thank you, you're kind." She couldn't quite keep the doubt out of the look she gave him. "About my phone call to St. Mawgan?"

"There's no hurry." He took her firmly by the elbow and led her to the foot of the blackwood staircase, where his housekeeper joined her, walking as if her shoes were soled with felt. She wore a tailored dark dress and there was a bunch of keys fixed to her belt. She looked at Janie and made no pretense of hiding her curiosity. Though her hair was silvery, her eyes were dark and lively. She looked every inch as Cornish as the master of the house, and it was a look that made Janie feel foreign with her fair skin and hair.

There was, she decided, almost a Latin look to these people.

"Please to step this way, miss."

Janie glanced once again at Pagan Pentrevah. She was about to insist on making her telephone call to Mrs. Burford when, with a rather curt inclination of his head, he turned on his heel and strode off down the hall where he vanished into the shadows.

Keys rattled as the housekeeper fingered them and Janie took the hint. She felt weary with hunger and it would be a relief to kick off her shoes and eat a quiet supper beside a warm fire.

"I'm coming," she said, and they walked up the stairs to a long gallery lined with family portraits. Janie tried not to feel as if she were being led to the tower to await the axman. What fanciful nonsense! Yet it was a house that lent itself to fancies and try as she would she couldn't rid herself of the feeling that Agatha with her bunch of keys was rather like a wardress in her severe dress and drawn-back hair.

"You all right, miss? You look a trifle pale."

"What I need," Janie said huskily, "is a nice cup of tea."

"You'll be having it, miss, as soon as you're settled in. Have you no belongings with you, if I might ask?"

"I had a suitcase but Mr. Pentrevah made me leave it in a bush. He brought me here on the saddle of his horse."

The housekeeper nodded as if to say it was the kind of thing he would do. "Expecting you we were, but we weren't sure when you'd be arriving. You're very welcome now you're here, miss."

Janie gazed at Agatha in astonishment. The housekeeper went on, "There's been a change in him ever since he came back from that trip he took to London. He's said nothing definite mind, but I've had the tower apartment ready and aired these past couple of weeks. I know the master, you can take it from me. I know when he's restless and there's something afoot. I've been part and parcel of this family a long time, miss."

Janie could well believe it, but the rest of what Agatha had said made little sense to her.

"As I say—" the housekeeper turned to face Janie at the foot of a narrow spiral stairway that presumably led to the tower apartment she had mentioned "—the master's been dropping hints about a visitor but he wouldn't commit himself. Soon as he set foot in this house after his return from London I saw a change in him and I said to myself then and there, he's met someone he has. Then that letter arrived with the London postmark and I hadn't a bit of doubt left in my mind that someone was coming on a visit—and here you are, miss!"

Janie gazed at the woman as if mesmerized. "But I—"

"I know he likes his little secrets," Agatha nodded wisely, "but he isn't going to be able to keep you a secret for long, now is he?"

"No," Janie said helplessly. She wanted to explain that she wasn't the expected visitor, but she couldn't seem to say the words. It was as if some mental block was preventing her from voicing the simple explanation that she was a stranger to Pagan Pentrevah and had met him for the first time less than an hour ago.

"Miss Tristana could tell there was something he was keeping to himself, so she went off in a huff to stay with friends of hers at Helston."

"Tristana?" It was a most evocative name Janie thought.

"His sister, miss."

"Oh...yes, his sister." Janie said it weakly, one of her hands clutching the rail of the stairs. "I do feel odd—"

"What you need is some good hot food inside you, miss." Agatha propelled her up the winding stairs to a door that she threw open with something of a flourish.

"You make yourself comfortable, miss, while I go and see about your supper and something for you to sleep in. Fancy dumping your suitcase in a bush! But I suppose we have to allow for the fact that it's been many a long year since he took an interest in a young lady.''

Agatha stood back and studied Janie. "And it's a wan-looking one you are right now. My word, talk about chalk and cheese, yet some folk say that men stick to what took their fancy as lads.''

With that the housekeeper made for the door and was about to close it when Janie found her voice. "Agatha?''

"Yes, miss?''

Janie ran her gaze around the tower bedroom. "It's circular,'' she said, and felt rather foolish considering all that she could have said. She just hadn't the energy to sort out the muddle she seemed to be getting into.

"In a round room, miss, there aren't any corners for the Devil to lurk in.'' The door closed and Janie felt the quietness of the tower close in around her, and whichever way she looked she seemed to see a man with black hair and spellbinding eyes.

LITTLE BLUE-EDGED FLAMES leaped along the logs as they burned slowly in the fireplace. Janie watched them as she sipped the delicious tea to which a generous tot of rum had been added. She was wrapped in a warm camel-colored robe that reached past her toes, an indication that the girl to whom it belonged was far taller than herself and no doubt took after her brother.

On a table beside her chair stood a tray of dishes from which drifted some inviting smells, but first she had to enjoy her tea and the sense of comfort it gave her as it moved through her body, bringing her gradually alive to the strange situation in which she found herself.

Why hadn't she protested when Agatha had taken her for Pagan Pentrevah's female visitor? Had it been her instinctive love of drama and mystery that had kept her from saying, "I barely know the man. We met on the moor, not in London, so he couldn't have been dropping hints about me."

The flames held Janie's gaze and the welcoming warmth stole around her and added to the unusual charm of the room in which she found herself so comfortably ensconced in a large floral-covered armchair. A pair of lamps diffused a warm and intimate glow and she breathed the scent of pomander balls on the wide expanse of the dressing table. There was also an immense, carved clothespress, deep rugs over the timbered floor, and an impossibly grand bed with a canopy and fringe attached to the tall carved posts, goat-legged imps running up and down them in vivid detail.

Needless to say Janie hadn't slept in such a room in her life. A room in a tower, with a bathroom converted from what would have been in days gone by an armory where weapons were kept so the house could be defended.

"The Towers isn't just a house," Agatha had said proudly after showing Janie the bathroom. "It's what we call in Cornwall a *plas* and it's been the home of the Pentrevahs since way back in time. It's a thing with the Pentrevah men that the *plas* should never fall into the hands of strangers."

"Yet he isn't married," Janie had said. No married man would be expecting a female guest, and he had said himself that he hadn't a wife.

"Mr. Pagan never had a *wife*," Agatha told her, a trifle mysteriously. "No doubt you'll be knowing the reason why."

Janie had longed to delve, and yet at the same time she had hesitated again to make it known that she wasn't Mr. Pagan's "young woman."

A little peeved with herself because she didn't quite understand her own behavior Janie examined the covered dishes on the tray. There was a delicious looking rabbit stew with dumplings, and to follow was a corner-shaped pie that smelled of spiced apples, a jug of cream on the side.

With a sigh of pleasure Janie tucked into the food and it had been a long time since food had tasted so good. The rabbit meat was white and meltingly tender and the dumplings were fluffy and tasty. Quite soon she had cleared the plate and was pouring cream on hot apple pie. It tasted heavenly, and when she sat back in her armchair, replete, Janie decided that it hadn't been too bad, after all, being found on the moor by Pagan Pentrevah. He was a hospitable host albeit a mysterious one. She wriggled her toes in the glow of the fire and felt steeped in the bodily well-being that comes after anxiety and the sating of hunger. Her eyes were pure green as they rested slumberously on the flame-licked logs; whatever the morning might bring, tonight she felt contented.

Janie was nodding off to sleep when a hand touched her shoulder and shook her awake. She gazed up dazedly into the hawkish eyes of her host. "Oh!" She sat up, pulling together the robe that had fallen open against the honey-colored silk of the nightdress Agatha had given her to wear.

"I startled you." He glanced at the empty dishes on the tray. "I see you had a good supper."

"It was excellent, thank you." She felt a tinge of heat in her cheeks, and she suspiciously asked herself what he wanted. His hand had withdrawn from her shoulder but his touch had left her tingling. He stood over her and made her feel lost and helpless in the deep armchair.

"I see that Agatha has fixed you up." His eyes swept her up and down. "You look a trifle lost in that robe."

"Your housekeeper said it belonged to your sister. She must be tall like you, Mr. Pentrevah."

"Yes. Like me, Tristana is Cornish from her mane of black hair down to her toes; she has ridden wild ponies since she was an infant and that kind of activity makes a girl athletic. She's also one devil of a fine swimmer. We're only half a mile from the sea, you know, even though we appear to be in the wilds. My land drops two hundred feet to Spanish Bay, which is all mine, as well."

"You talk like a land-proud man." Janie gazed up at him and saw that he had changed out of his riding clothes and was wearing a corduroy smoking jacket the color of claret. She also noticed in that moment that he was carrying a decanter and a pair of stemmed glasses.

"I thought you might fancy a glass of wine," he said. "I usually have one, or two, about this time, and it's the genuine kind that I have shipped over from Oporto. I have a cousin in the business."

The wine glowed through the cut glass of the decanter, but Janie wasn't certain if it would be quite wise of her to accept his offer. "Come," he was quick to notice her hesitation. "A good rabbit stew deserves a glass of the best wine to chase it down. You will join me, Jane?"

"If you insist—"

"I insist on nothing," he began to fill the glasses. "I'm not out to coerce you, Jane."

"Thank you," she accepted the glass he handed her, her gaze following him as he moved to the fireplace and stood there, his broad back resting against the mantel. He raised his glass and watched her over the rim as he swallowed deeply. God, how big and dark he was! Her toes curled themselves in the long hem of the camel robe, aware as she had been on the moor of a vital, elemental quality in this man that, like a moorland gale, could sweep people off their feet. Because he had always lived in the wilds he was an untamed force.... A man in a position to have his own way when he wanted it.

She ducked her head to the glass in her hand and took a gulp of the wine. It rushed tingling and rich down her throat, making her gasp, and then she felt it in her veins like mercury.

"Good, eh?" His voice had softened and made her think of thunder and velvet. Good Lord, the wine had gone to her brain!

"Excellent," she agreed. "I'm sure you wouldn't put anything but the best wine in your cellars."

"Ah, even in a batch of wine there can be a bottle that looks perfect but can be poisonous. You can't always judge from appearances, that's the problem."

"Are you trying to judge me, Mr. Pentrevah?"

"What makes you ask me that, Jane?"

She gave a slight shrug and noticed again that he chose deliberately not to call her Janie. Nearly everyone she knew called her Janie, but the fact was that she had always preferred the plain simplicity of Jane. "You have those kind of eyes, I suppose. Vigilant, like a hawk getting ready to swoop on a hare."

"And you regard yourself as the hare I'm about to swoop on?" He gave a slightly derisive laugh. "Having regaled you with wine and lowered your defenses I

then carry you to the four-poster and have my will of
you until the dawn light comes streaking through the
windows? My dear young woman, you do have a lurid
imagination, not to mention quite a dash of conceit.
Why the devil should I fancy you?''

"I never for one moment—''

"Didn't you?'' His eyes mocked her discomfiture.
"That's all you've had in your head since the moment
we collided on the moor. You keep asking yourself
what I want of you, don't you, Jane?''

She stared up at him, held by his eyes and unable to
deny his assertion. "Your housekeeper said something rather odd,'' she said at last. "Agatha seemed to
mistake me for someone else you've been expecting.''

"You could have put her wise, couldn't you?'' His
eyes narrowed as he searched Janie's face. "What
stopped you? I know you didn't correct her because
when she came to tell me you'd been made comfortable, she referred to you as my 'young woman.' ''

"Yes, that's how she's been referring to me—''

"As I say, Jane, you could have told her that you
were nothing of the sort. It intrigues me that you
didn't deny her assumption.''

"I-I suppose I felt too worn out to bother.'' Janie
looked self-bewildered. "Why didn't you correct
her?''

"Because it suits me that Agatha should believe
that you're here because I invited you.''

"I really don't understand....'' The flush had re-
ceded from Janie's face and suddenly she looked
rather pale. Her eyes had gone from green to gray as
they did when she was tense and uncertain.

"Come, drink your wine,'' he urged. "I'm not
some sinister lord of the manor who intends you any

dire harm, but I do have a proposition to put to you and I would prefer that you didn't look at me as if I'd just suggested that we rob a bank together!''

Janie caught her breath, vagrantly amused by his irony but too on edge to smile. She decided to drink all the wine in her glass; it might be better at this precise moment to be slightly tipsy rather than sober. She suspected that already she had allowed herself to be drawn halfway into a risqué situation. She wasn't exactly scared but she could feel her own nervous tension.

She downed the wine and felt the soothing glow that stole through her body; it felt good but she couldn't allow herself to relax in this man's company.

"Is that better?" he queried. "Would you like another glass?"

"It's strong stuff," she shook her head. "I'd fall asleep on you."

"I wouldn't want that to happen." He half turned toward the fire and gazed down into the warm red heart of it, his profile firm and definite, the bold outline of his nose matching the strong jaw. The smoking jacket he wore was perfectly cut to his large frame, his shirt was flawlessly white against his swarthy skin. There was a look of brooding power about him as he stood as if lost in his thoughts, a clock held by two bronze horses ticking away the seconds above his dark head.

Janie found herself wondering how old he was. There wasn't a gleam of gray in his hair yet she sensed that he was close to forty, which seemed many moons removed from her own age. He certainly intrigued her, and alerted her to the basic differences between the male and the female. She told herself he had a strong dash of the Cornish smuggler in his veins, a deep affinity with the moors, and possibly a wild streak of passion.

Pagan Pentrevah.... How well the name suited him!

"I'm going to ask you something that you may resent," he finally said. "I expect you'll jump down my throat but it's essential that you give me a candid answer. Have I your word?"

"Not until I have your question," she fenced.

"Are you in love with anyone?"

Janie felt the breath catch in her throat. "I don't see that it's any of your business— Why on earth should it matter to you whether I'm in love or not?"

He turned deliberately to face her. "Because I need you to pretend that you're in love with me," he said distinctly.

CHAPTER THREE

HE HADN'T STRUCK HER as the sort of man to talk nonsense, but what he had just said was utter nonsense. "You're joking of course?" she said.

"I was never more serious." And he looked it, not a vestige of humor showing in his face, least of all in his eyes that dwelt upon her so intently.

Janie swallowed dryly and wished she had accepted that second glass of wine. If the first glass had made her slightly tipsy, then his remark had certainly sobered her. "Why are you suggesting such a pretense? It's crazy! Beyond reason!"

"I have my reason, Jane, don't be in any doubt of that. I'm not some sort of mad recluse who goes around saying that sort of thing, if you're wondering."

"I certainly was wondering—and why pick on me?"

"You said you were an actress and I'm offering you the best role you're going to get this side of the Tamar."

"I act in plays, Mr. Pentrevah, opposite actors. What you're proposing is an act of...of deceit and I wouldn't know my lines!"

"I'd expect you to invent them. You're a woman, Jane, and women are deuced good at faking a wide range of emotions."

"For what purpose?" Janie still couldn't believe in

the reality of this scene. It was more farfetched than some of those in the repertory plays she had appeared in; melodrama that rarely made it into the West End because it was so romantically absurd and producers felt that sophisticated audiences would laugh.

Janie wished right now that she could laugh.

"Before I launch into details, Jane, I have to know if there's some young actor in your life? Someone who might take it into his head to come looking for you?"

Instantly Janie was tempted to launch into a lie, a description of some dashing Adonis who was very possessive of her. It seemed such an easy thing to do but even as she urged herself to speak, she was shaking her head in answer to his query, as if he forcibly willed the truth from her with his spellbinding eyes.

"So you're a free agent, Jane?"

"Not at all," she replied. "I have a job to go to."

"With an elderly lady who'll expect you to fetch and carry for her?"

Janie felt cornered by his eyes, certain she hadn't mentioned the purpose of her job with Mrs. Burford. "How do you know that?" Her voice faded and she could feel her heart beating at the bars of her ribs.

"Mere observation," he drawled. "There aren't many offices or shops in St. Mawgan, and somehow I can't picture you behind a counter or a typewriter. You have a certain air of breeding, Jane. You're well spoken and you spoke of your grandmother with respect as well as affection. You strike me as the type to take on a companion's job, for the time being. You are the kind of girl an elderly woman of means would put her trust in."

"Your cleverness, Mr. Pentrevah, must often delight you." Jane wasn't often sarcastic but somehow he induced it, along with some other reactions she wasn't familiar with.

"It's a habit with moorland people to observe.... I said there were bogs around, didn't I?"

"You did," she agreed. "Right now I feel as if I'm being dragged into one."

"Really?" He quirked a black eyebrow. "I felt that it showed an adventurous streak that you should leave the road and venture onto the moor."

"And from what you've said I would say that what you need is an adventuress, and I'm not one of those, Mr. Pentrevah!"

"Perhaps you're afraid your acting ability wouldn't be up to the task of faking love for me?" He looked as sardonic as he sounded. "Perhaps that's why you're out of work as regards the theater, Miss Larue. You're a lousy actress, is that it?"

"No I'm not!" She was stung where it hurt. "I'm a very good actress if you must know, but I don't go around bragging about it."

"Oh, but you should, Jane. The best way to get on is to learn how to blow your own trumpet, but if you're going to be modest about yourself then others are going to accept that you're a mouse."

"I-I have some fairly good press clippings of my work." Her eyes stung a little and she hated him for bringing her near to tears with his brutal frankness. "I know I can act but it's getting the right part that's important."

"So in the meantime you're going to play drudge to this elderly lady, is that it?"

"You know how to lay on the whip, don't you?" Temper as well as tears shimmered in Janie's eyes.

"Hell's fire, girl, don't look at me like that! I'm not asking you to sell your soul to Satan!" His eyes impaled her where she sat. His features were hard, hammered from living bronze. His mouth was made for the kind of speech that was never anything but direct and demanding. "I'm actually giving you the chance to carry on your occupation. Why, you should be a veritable Bernhardt after playing the role of my lady-love."

Janie crouched down in the armchair, as if his amazing proposition had turned her bones to butter.

"There's a salary attached, as well," he drawled. "I don't expect you to work at such a task unpaid. I'll add twenty pounds a week to what the good lady at St. Mawgan was going to give you."

Janie started to shake her head, and then hesitated. She wasn't mercenary but money was always a consideration for someone who didn't have any. Her bank account had almost staggered to a halt and financial desperation had driven her to accept this post with Mrs. Burford.

"For how long would I be expected to ... to pretend what you ask of me?" she asked him huskily.

"For as long as it takes, Jane."

"What is the object?" Her eyes looked huge, the green in them battling with the gray. "The whole thing sounds utterly crazy!"

"So you said before, Jane, but in a manner of speaking life itself is a strange kettle of fish. Look at it this way, perhaps you were meant to have that flat tire on the way to this dreary job of listening to the memoirs of an old lady and possibly taking her little dog for walks. I think I might safely say that my conversation has some virility in it, and my dogs are Great Danes—hounds of the Baskervilles."

He smiled down at Janie with brief amusement, but

behind that smile his look held the essence of challenge.

"Running scared?" he mocked.

"It isn't every night, Mr. Pentrevah, that a girl is asked to be a man's fake fiancée."

"You have it slightly wrong, Jane. I'm asking you to act as my wife."

He hadn't really said that, Janie told herself. Tiredness, a strange house and a glass of strong wine had affected her hearing.

"You're taking it very matter-of-factly," he said.

"Because this time, Mr. Pentrevah, you've got to be kidding."

"I assure you, Jane, that everything we've talked about in this room tonight is of the utmost seriousness to me. I don't go in for schoolboy humor. The job, and we'll call it that for the sake of your sanity, demands that you pose in this house as the mistress of it, or would you find the role too demanding for your talents?"

"I'm wondering where you'd find someone crazy enough to accept your proposition, Mr. Pentrevah."

"I expect there are agencies that hire out women for all sorts of activities, but you happened to come along and the beauty of it is that you have experience as an actress." Abruptly he moved from the fireplace and leaned over her, his hands gripping the arms of her chair. His gaze dominated her and her reaction to his sudden closeness was acutely disturbing. In the course of her stage work she had been held in the arms of some really good-looking actors, but this dark, far from handsome man made her feel at his mercy.

"Accept it as a dare." The words seemed to purr in his throat.

"Y-you must need someone very badly—" Her lips trembled around the words and she could feel herself shrinking in every nerve in case he touched her.

"The money's good, Jane. You should be able to save quite a bit of your salary as you won't be paying any board or lodging. I expect money is quite a consideration for a young actress. Think, Jane, a little nest egg will save you in future from having to take employment as a companion."

"It might be dull, Mr. Pentrevah, but at least it's...safe."

"You think I'd be dangerous?"

"I don't think," she rejoined, "I know!"

"You're that good at judging men?" he mocked, as skeptical as he had every right to look considering how unworldly Janie looked, curled up in an armchair in a robe a couple of sizes too large for her. "You and I have only known each other a short while."

"And I'm supposed to accept your proposition in a couple of minutes. I'd need time to think it over."

"Dammit, girl, what is there to think over? You need a job and I'm offering you one. I thought I saw in you some spirit and a lively sense of curiosity." He touched with a finger the silver bracelet on her wrist, Gothic in design. "I took you for a girl who believes in fatalism, exorcism and other mystic rites. Am I wrong?"

"Why do you mention exorcism?" She met his gaze, like that of a hawk in ruthless pursuit of its prey.

"Strange you should ask." He straightened to his full height and his face had a distant look. "Perhaps what I have in mind is related to exorcism, the bringing in of something puritan in order to offset the forces of something profane."

Janie couldn't take her eyes from his face. A cold

thrill went up and down her spine. "You say the most maddening things— Now what is that remark supposed to mean?"

"The way it sounds." His gaze swooped down upon her and pinned her to her seat. "You're a virgin, aren't you?"

"H-how dare you?" Janie felt as if he had stripped her for the evidence.

"Don't look so outraged. I'm not proposing that I should rob you of such a precious jewel. You may safely save it for when you fall in love...you will, Jane. Most women are looking for love, some with tenderness, others with calculation. All I ask of you is that you live in my house for a few weeks and appear devoted to me. Hell's fire, do you find me so dark and dour—so impossible to love, even though it will be a game of pretense?"

"It would have to be only a pretense." Because he had such an overwhelming effect on her Janie had to shield her feelings by being offhand. She didn't want to believe there had been a flare of pain in his ebony and gold eyes when he had spoken of himself in relation to love.

"It is only a game," he assured her. "The stakes are in your favor in a financial sense but I hope to pull off a coup of my own. Come, let me persuade you."

The softening diminuendo of his voice, the almost seducing tone made her all the more wary of him. This was a man who could, if he set out to do so, evoke a sweeping emotional response from a woman. Janie had to face this even as she calculated that the money he offered was good and with such a salary each week she could replenish her starving bank account and build up a reserve for the future.

A glance around this comfortably appointed bedroom was enough to inform her that Pagan Pentrevah was an affluent man. He owned a great house and land, and for some personal reason he wished to convince someone that he was married.

It was decidedly odd but Janie could feel herself succumbing to the idea.

"There would be no question—" she bit her lip "—what I mean is, you wouldn't expect...reality?"

"No, only romance," was his casual reply.

"Romance?" she gasped.

"In the truest sense of the term, Jane. Words these days are already losing all original meaning as they become twisted by minds made base to match the cheap convolutions. Romance, my girl, means the marvelous, the mysterious, the fanciful. We play at love without making it—you have read the Brontës, no doubt?"

"Of course."

"There's no 'of course' about it, Jane, not these far from salubrious days. Girls are weaned on garbage-pail fiction, not the great tales of chivalry and drama.... Who decided to name you Jane, or is Jane Larue a name you invented for the stage?"

"No, it's my real name."

"And what goes with it?"

"I'm Jane Emily."

"Ah, don't you see?"

"Do I?" She swallowed. "Am I supposed to regard you as Heathcliff?"

"I prefer that it be Rochester."

"Oh, really, this is such nonsense!"

"It's my way of trying to convince you that our relationship will be no more than a fiction."

"Are you a good actor, Mr. Pentrevah?"

"Life teaches us to hide our true selves, Jane, and that is a form of acting is it not?"

"So when I look at you I'm not seeing the real Pagan Pentrevah but a man who is hiding his true self?"

"You are seeing, Jane, more of me than I have shown to a good many people. I've confronted you with myself because I need your assistance. Can I take it that I have it?"

"Can I ask if there's a special person for whom we act out this...melodrama?"

"I've been expecting that query, Jane, and the answer is yes."

"Is it a woman, Mr. Pentrevah?"

He inclined his dark head and she saw a flicker of fire in his eyes; a glint of danger deep inside them. Her senses warned her that it wasn't wise to probe but she felt a strong inclination to do so. After all, she would have a starring role in this production.

"Agatha told me you hadn't a wife—"

"I also told you that, Jane."

"Yes, but I'm not sure I can trust you."

"I'm well aware that you distrust me." He sought around in his pockets and drew out his well-thumbed cheroot case. "Do you mind if I smoke—this is your bedroom and I'm mindful of the fact."

Janie detected an underlying note of meaning in his voice and her heart gave a jolt. What did he intend to do about the bedroom situation if she agreed to his outlandish proposal that she live at the Towers and pretend she was married to him?

He lighted his cheroot at her murmur of acquiescence. The aromatic smoke twined around his head and his brooding features, and Janie was struck by the intimacy of this moment, of a man smoking in her bedroom and looking at her in her nightwear. She wasn't a prude but she was a girl who hadn't until now allowed any man the privilege of such an intimacy, which the ruby-shaded lamps intensified, casting a rubescent glow over the turned-back sheets and lace counterpane of the big bed.

Janie had glanced toward the bed before she could stop herself, and then she prayed that Pagan Pentrevah hadn't noticed and read what was going through her mind.

"Yes," he drawled, "the plot raises one or two problems, doesn't it?"

She didn't dare look at him and felt herself go hot all over. "What do you intend to do about...that side of things?" The question sounded horribly coy but it had to be asked.

"I'll be frank with you, Jane." He flicked ash into the fireplace. "The woman I intend to delude is insatiably curious about other women and if I don't share an adjoining room with you, then she'll take it that I don't share anything else. You take my meaning?"

She nodded. Only too well did she take his meaning and this time a sweeping heat rose out of her nightdress and licked at her hairline. Even the thought of fictional lovemaking with this man made her burn; she didn't dare to imagine what the reality would be like.

"Are you—is she someone you're in love with—or the reverse?" Janie just had to ask. "Is she married to someone else, is that it?"

"My dear girl, Roxanne was married to me."

"But—" Janie gave him a bewildered look. "I was told you never had a wife."

"Nor had I." He said it with infinite irony. "Roxanne was everything but a wife, and we were declared unmarried a long time ago."

"That's an odd way of putting it, Mr. Pentrevah. Don't you like to call it divorce?"

"We never were divorced!" He started to pace the

room, back and forth, the smoke of his cheroot erupting around his head. His stride was almost animal, almost savage, as if he were filled with a smoldering anger that was rising to the surface.

"Roxanne and I were married a year when she vanished from my life—vanished in a way that made people suspect I had killed her. A bracelet of hers was found near Prowler's Pool. I had given it to her so I knew it well, apart from which there was an inscription inside. The police were suspicious, but I knew Roxanne wasn't in the bog. I knew her, too well! She wanted to discredit me and she managed so well there was talk of an official inquiry to try and establish my guilt. Finally it was decided there was no substantial evidence on which to base a trial. Nevertheless a lot of people believed I was responsible for her disappearance and, though none of the Pentrevahs have ever pretended to be angels, it sticks in the throat like a hook to be whispered about as a wife killer."

He paused upon that evocative word and studied Jane, who tried not to let it show on her face how shocked she felt by his revelation. Was it possible that in a fit of rage he had tried to kill Roxanne for some reason?

In Janie's opinion he looked as if he could lose his temper pretty thoroughly, as if all his passions were as strong as the moorland wind and deep as the sea that beat against the shoreline rocks.

"At the end of seven years I applied to have my marriage declared null and void. I was free of her—or so I thought!"

With these words he flung the stub of his cheroot into the fire. It was a violent gesture, as if he craved to burn out the memories that had bitten so deep into his mind, and possibly his heart.

"Well, Jane, have you nothing to say?" His gaze brooded upon her. "Are you shocked?"

"I am puzzled. Why do you need to produce a phony wife—you're rid of her, aren't you?"

He took a deep breath. "I happen to know that Roxanne is returning to this part of the world and, quite simply, I wish to spike her guns."

It was Janie's turn to catch her breath. "She...she's coming back into your life?"

"Yes, by hell!" He kicked at a smoldering log and it broke in a spate of sparks that shot up the cavernous chimney.

"After the way she treated you?"

"Yes, she has her gall, hasn't she?"

"People truly believed you'd pushed her into the bog?"

"I expect you'd have believed it, as well. I think you've had me tapped as the Devil himself ever since I brought you here, but contrary to what you think, the Devil is a woman. The most beautiful witch you'll ever see in this life, and she'll be coming here to the Towers to flaunt herself and, by hell, I want to show her that I'm no longer free to fall under her damned spell!"

"So I'm to be the amulet that keeps your witch at bay?" Janie gave a tremulous smile and moved an expressive hand down her body. "Do you really think I have the equipment?"

"You'll do," he said curtly. "If I searched up and down the country I wouldn't find another to match Roxanne so I'm going to take advantage of the stroke of luck that made you and I meet on the moor just as I was racking my brain for a way to deal with her."

"Why are you so sure she's coming back to Cornwall?" Janie wasn't vain but her feelings were rather

stung by the ready way he agreed that she was no
match for the remarkable Roxanne, this one-time
wife of his who had walked out on him and left a
cloud of suspicion hanging over his head.

"About a month ago I received an unsigned letter
informing me of her whereabouts in London. As the
letter was written in block capitals in order to disguise
the handwriting I surmised she had sent it and was up
to one of her tricks. Well, if she fondly imagines she's
going to put me through the hoop again, then she's in
for a letdown. I went to London myself to do a little
checking. One afternoon I saw her emerge from the
hotel mentioned in the letter. She hadn't changed—
she still had hair like a flame and the long silky legs I
used to chase through the heather.... It was in the
heather on the moor that we often allowed our feelings to run away with us."

He ran his eyes over Janie's intent face. "Do I
shock you?"

"Not in the least," she lied. It wasn't the lovemaking in the heather that shocked her, it was the look
she had caught sight of in his eyes...the smoldering
embers of an experience that tied him to Roxanne
even as he sought to be free of her.

He couldn't forget her beauty, nor her response to
him where the grasshoppers clicked in the hot sun and
where the earth smelled rich and loamy.

"If you and I, Jane, are to carry out this *folie à deux*,
then it's best that you know everything. Roxanne and
I loved in the heather and made our child there....
The child she didn't want and had taken away from
her before it could be born. I had my hands around
her neck the night I found out, and that was why she
ran out on me and left even my family to suspect me
of violence toward her."

He drew a deep harsh breath. "There it is, Jane, in all its raw truth. Do you blame me for using an extreme method to keep her from shaking up my life again? Will you help me?"

"You ask me that," Janie said quietly, "but I can't help wondering if you're still in love with her. I'm sure you were once crazy about her, weren't you?"

"I was besotted with her," he admitted. "Maybe the virus is still in my blood, but I don't want her back! She killed whatever respect I had for her. I despise her!"

"You want her exorcised," Janie murmured.

"I'd like to try." A cynical smile twisted his lips. "I'd like to see the pure and the profane come face to face. It should be quite an experience."

"I haven't said—" Janie drew a troubled sigh. "Won't you let me sleep on it?"

He took several dragging moments to consider her plea, then finally he inclined his head. "Very well, but don't let it give you a nightmare so that in the morning you'll beg me to let you go to this elderly lady in St. Mawgan."

He gave Janie a look that took her in from her tousled hair to her bare toes. "Let me just say this, Jane. I wanted my child and she got someone to take it away and she threw in my face that it was a boy. From way back, since the first Pentrevah was a Cornish warlord there have been sons to carry on the Pentrevah name. I could have killed Roxanne for robbing me of my son and I came close to it.... Next time I'll do it!"

The breath dragged through him, and then abruptly he bent over Janie and taking hold of her left hand he carried it to his lips and kissed it. "Thank you for listening to me, Jane. Have a good night's sleep."

The bedroom door closed behind him and Janie allowed herself to give way to the weakness she felt, as if she had been buffeted by a high wave that had taken away her breath and left her stranded and out of her depth. She had just listened to a story of love and violence and she didn't doubt for a moment that every word of it was true.

This stranger from out of the night had revealed the intimate and painful facts of his broken marriage. And, because the shards of it were still stabbing him he asked her, a stranger to him, to pose as his wife in order to offset the fascination she knew he still felt for Roxanne... flame haired, enticing and cruel.

"I can't do it!" Janie rocked in the armchair as if she had an unspecified pain. "I won't do it!"

Yet even as she whispered the words the dark image of Pagan Pentrevah was more vivid in her mind than people she had ate and acted with and known for weeks during the run of a play.

He was nothing to her, yet he had this hold upon her.

A charred log broke apart and the sound set her nerves on edge. She glanced around the tower bedroom and seemed to hear the voice of Agatha again.

"In a circular room, miss, there aren't any corners for the Devil to lurk in."

Janie had the distinct feeling that Agatha was mistaken.

CHAPTER FOUR

JANIE WOKE ABRUPTLY from a deep and surprisingly dreamless sleep. She lay basking for a few mindless moments in the warmth and comfort of a bed that couldn't be the hard and lumpy thing at her lodgings in London. She stretched luxuriously and slowly turned her gaze to the sunlight coming through the windows, long casements with brocade draperies at either side of them.

Gradually the dazedness of sleep faded away and she became aware of a rather heavy weight across her legs.

"What on earth?" She half sat up and gazed in astonishment at the great dog that lay snoozing across her legs. At her movement he raised his large head and Janie felt a stab of alarm. The animal was a Great Dane, gray in color and big as a donkey. He gazed back at her with a profound solemnity and Janie could only hope that he was tamer than he looked.

"Good morning to you, boy." She remembered what her host had told her, that he had a pair of Great Danes, but he hadn't warned her that one of them liked to take a nap on a visitor's bed.

A ray of sunlight winking in the silver of a pot caught her attention and there on a tray on the bedside table was a teapot, a cup and saucer, milk jug and sugar bowl. Bless Agatha! Janie hadn't enjoyed tea in

bed for a long time, not since she had to go home to
Grandma Polly with a racking cold caught in a drafty
Leeds theater.

"Stir yourself, old chap." She moved onto her side.
"I'm longing for a cup of tea and you may have a
biscuit. Here, do you like shortbreads?"

He caught the biscuit between his teeth and it was
gone in an instant. He watched her with lazy attention
as she poured out her tea in a rather nice china cup
with a ring of roses around it. There was no getting
away from it, the house of Pentrevah was certainly a
place of strange and wonderful surprises.

Mmm, sheer nectar! Janie sipped her tea and snug-
gled her shoulders into the big downy pillows. She'd
enjoy for a little while longer the luxury of the four-
poster, then she'd be up and away. Her decision was
that it was safer to go and work for Mrs. Burford...even if the job proved less dramatic.

Suddenly the dog stirred and for all its size leaped
gracefully from the bed to the floor. He ambled across
to the door that a moment later was opened by Agatha
who bustled in carrying a pair of suitcases, which she
placed on a stool at the foot of the bed.

"Here you are, madam. Mr. Pagan went out early
himself to attend to your car and to bring it home for
you. Are the suitcase keys in your handbag, madam,
so I can unpack for you?"

Janie blinked her lashes and what was uppermost in
her mind was that Agatha had ceased to address her as
"miss" and was now referring to her as "madam."

"Slept deep, did you?" Agatha stood there considering Janie in the impossibly grand bed. "My, you
look no more than a child, yet it's a married woman
that you are. Himself told me. I knew he was up to

something but I could have been knocked over with a feather when he came out with it, that you met sudden like in London and—"

"He told you *what*?" Janie sat up as if an electric current had shot through her body. "How could he...he promised—"

"Promised to keep it a secret?" Agatha's features relaxed into a smile. "It was bound to come out, madam, now you're here at the Towers with him. I mean, I could hardly move you into the Black Baron Tower without a bit of talk, and there's Miss Tristana to consider. There was enough of a scandal when she was but a schoolgirl, so it wouldn't be kind to let her think that you and Mr. Pagan were carrying on and not properly churched for it. I know you've been on the stage, madam, and such folks are a bit unorthodox."

"Unorthodox!" Janie gasped. "Let me inform you that Mr. Pagan and I—"

"What's this about you and I Jane?" He strolled into the bedroom as if on cue, big and easy in a cashmere sweater and whipcord trousers, his black hair ruffled from the moorland winds. His eyes fixed Janie above Agatha's head and there was a look in them that dared her to defy him.

"You had no right—"

"I had every right, my dear." He came with deliberate strides to the bed, lowered himself to the unoccupied side and reached over to enfold Janie in his powerful arms.

"I know we spoke about letting people think we were just good friends for a while, but upon consideration, darling, I decided it was for the best to bare our bosoms." As he spoke his gaze slid down to where the too big nightdress had fallen open to disclose that part of Janie's anatomy. Feeling his eyes upon her, she blushed to suit the storm going on inside her.

"Let me go!"

"Come, little one, Agatha will think I've got myself a young termagant for a bride if you don't stop sulking."

"I could kill you!" Janie spoke through gritted teeth. "You're arrogant and audacious, and I wish I'd never set eyes on you!"

"Her mood will get sweeter as the day goes on." He shot a pained smile at his housekeeper, as if to imply that new brides could be a bit of a headache. "She's really quite a placid child, and rather pretty, don't you think, Agatha?"

Agatha stood there and looked at him as if she thought he had gone a trifle senile, getting himself mixed up with an actress from London half his age.

"Aye, she has the Celt eyes and the skin like baby's milk." Agatha emphasized the word baby. "Would you like me to unpack for you, madam, or shall I see to it later?"

"Later." It was Pagan Pentrevah who replied. "We'll take breakfast in the flower room as it's a sunny morning, but right now I'd like a few minutes alone with my wife."

Janie tensed as if to leap out of his arms and at once they tightened around her and he very conclusively silenced her by bringing his lips down hard upon hers. In the swooning distance Janie heard the Great Dane shooed from the room and the closing of the door behind the housekeeper, who went off believing the lie Pagan Pentrevah had told her without a scrap of conscience.

His lips held Janie's and his body forced her to recline against the pillows, where he held her as his mouth slid to her collarbone. "There was no other way," his mouth moved against her bare skin. "I knew you wouldn't agree to what I asked of you, so I had to force the issue. Come, it won't be as bad as you imagine. You can console yourself with the thought that you don't really belong to an arrogant, audacious bully like me."

"Thank heaven!" Janie's glare of rebellion concealed a nervousness she wouldn't admit to; he was too close to her for comfort and she could actually smell the tang of the moors on him. "Agatha told me you had seen to my car and brought it back to the Towers."

"Yes, aren't you going to thank me?"

"You have to be joking!" She thrust a hand against his shoulder and felt a muscle smooth as steel and just as unlikely to bend; her heart quaked at the touch of him, he felt so strong and unyielding. "Y-you haven't played fair, Mr. Pentrevah, you led me to believe I could make my own decision but you obviously meant to have your own way."

"I couldn't let you slip out of my grasp, Jane. I could tell that you'd choose to be an old lady's companion rather than my conspirator. Look at it from this point of view, life is going to demand that you take risks so you might as well take one that will put cash in your pocket. Where's the harm?"

"In the deceit involved. In having to tell your sister such an outrageous lie. Is it necessary to do that?"

"I fear so. No one knows Roxanne as I do, the way she can turn on the charm and use enticement as if she invented it. She'll try her tricks on Tristana so I think it's best if only you and I, Jane, are privy to the deception. Come, it's only a game—"

"A game of chance," Janie exclaimed. "Roxanne has already proved that she can be treacherous."

"You aren't timid, are you, Jane?" His eyes blatantly mocked her. "You won't go far as an actress if you're afraid to take a gamble.... I'd say that you've chosen a very tough and demanding profession for a girl. I expect you've already come up against a few wolves."

"None of them more conniving than you, Mr. Pentrevah."

"You must start to call me Pagan."

"The name certainly suits you, inside and out."

"I'm glad you think so." Then before Janie could resist him, he had gripped her by the chin and was taking stock of her face, and taking his time about it. "With your hair like that you look like a page from out of King Arthur's court."

"Sorry I'm not a devastating beauty." Janie resented the feel of his fingers and the possessive way they gripped her. Her toes curled at the very thought of what she was getting into...of what she was in already, a four-poster bed upon which she was helplessly held by this man.

"You're no beauty," he agreed, "but you have a certain piquant quality."

"You're not exactly handsome yourself, Mr. Pentrevah."

"The sooner you start calling me Pagan the better."

"I haven't said that I'm going through with this preposterous nonsense of pretending to be your wife."

"I could make you, do you realize that?" His hand slid meaningly down her slim neck to where the nightdress gaped. "Are your origins Celtic?"

"My mother was Welsh, if that qualifies."

"You speak of her in the past tense."

"She was working as a nurse in London and was traveling home one weekend to my grandparents' farm when the bus went out of control and crashed down a hillside. Several of the passengers were killed or injured—my mother died on the way to hospital. She was twenty-four."

"Ah, that was tragic for you, Jane."

"I know. I was an infant at the time but I remember her. I-I loved seeing her in her nurse's cape with the scarlet lining."

"What of your father?"

"I can't say." Janie glanced away from the intent eyes. "He was a drifter. I can't remember much about him so he must have drifted out of our lives when I was a baby. I rarely think about him. It's as if he's dead, as well."

"Poor Jane."

The words were spoken with genuine feeling but Janie was resolved not to let Pagan Pentrevah get under her skin. "I've managed to fill up my life and I'm ambitious," she rejoined. "I'm going to make it as an actress."

"You'll get plenty of practice in the coming weeks."

When he said that Janie felt an urge to defy him, but when she met his eyes she saw again what she had glimpsed last night. The angry torment of a man who desired a woman whom in his heart he despised for what she had done to their child; who by now would be riding the moors with him, climbing the cliffs and sailing upon the waters of the bay.

He needed desperately, Janie saw that, to be able to confront Roxanne with a fait accompli. He wanted to show her that he had been able to live—and love—without her.

"You're giving me an old-fashioned look, Jane," he said. "What's your verdict?"

"I've never seen a more likely candidate for male dominance, yet you allow a woman to panic you into a deception involving another woman. How come?"

"We all have our Achilles' heel," he said sardonically. "It would appear that Roxanne is mine. I don't trust her, and I don't trust myself where she's concerned. You see, Jane, we knew each other as boy and girl. Everyone said we were made for each other. Our marriage was celebrated on a midsummer's eve when the bonfires were lighted on Carn Brea across country to St. Agnes Beacon. It's a pagan festival to drive away evil and promote good fortune; in the old days the fires were lighted to ward off witchcraft.... To this day I can see Roxanne's face as she stood there in her white velvet dress and the rising flames lighted her up!"

He breathed deeply and sat up away from Jane, his arm slackening from around her. "Like a moonstruck fool I thought I'd married the most exciting girl in the whole of Cornwall but in truth I'd married a witch. My best man, Hunt Lincoln, did a sketch of her and I saw it a few days later. He had drawn her with tiny flames licking at her hair and playing around her temples, and he had managed to capture in her eyes what I didn't see until the night she brazenly admitted that she had had our child taken out of her body. It was exactly a year to the day we married; it was as if she had waited to give the boy in sacrifice to the devil fires burning inside her."

He stood up and paced to the windows, where he stood with his back to the sunlight, his face in shadow. "We had the most colossal row in the bedroom I'd let her furnish like the boudoir of a whore! There was a party going on in the great hall and when I struck her, she screamed so everyone heard her. Later that same night she left the Towers. She crept away like a cat in the dark and nothing more was seen of her until the police found her bracelet, the one she'd been wearing with the new dress she had bought for the party. It was the style of the dress that started the row we had; I knew she was carrying but as soon as she appeared in that damn dress I guessed she'd had something done to herself.... Her figure was like a girl's again, like it had been on the eve of our wedding.

"I could have flung her down the stairs," he said, the fury banked down in his voice. "I wish to heaven I had!"

Janie couldn't take her eyes away from him, so big and somehow unassailable, and yet so very hurt deep inside.

"I'm not saying all this in order to appeal to your tender mercies Jane. It's a brute of a story but I want you to know that my need of you is greater than that of the old lady whose ennui needs an outlet in a young companion. I won't expect you to read historical novels to me, or to walk my hounds, but I shall ask you to act my wife as if there's an award in it for you. Are you going to?"

"All right." It was as if some stranger inside herself spoke the words that committed her to the intrigue. In her mind Janie was appalled by the step she was taking...a step deep as Prowler's Pool where Roxanne had left her bracelet to brand her husband as a murderer. The very thought of the woman sent a shiver through Janie.

"I'm grateful." Pagan Pentrevah came back to the bedside and took Janie's hands in his. "Ah, you feel cold! What you need is a good breakfast inside you.

Get dressed and come downstairs, I'll be waiting for you."

Janie gazed up at him. "I've never done anything like this before in my life.... I hope nothing will go wrong."

He pressed her hands almost painfully between his own. "It's a desperate measure I know, and we still know so very little about each other, but for better or worse a couple has to learn about each other after a real marriage. This is no more of a *folie à deux* than any real marriage, and I speak from painful experience. Get dressed, and remember when you come downstairs to call me Pagan. Practice the name a few times."

She lay huddled in the bed as if it were the only safe place in the house. Her eyes looking enormous as she peered over the bedspread at him, the big dark stranger whom she had promised to treat like a husband.

"Don't be all day," he said, and was gone.

Oh, Lord, Janie curled her toes together as a tingle of apprehension swept through her. She felt as she did when she waited in the wings for the curtain to rise, knowing that any minute she must step out on the stage and become not herself but someone invented by another person—a person who had to convince the audience of her reality.

That was what she must do in this case, regard the Towers as a theater, its rooms as a stage setting, its occupants as the audience, and Pagan Pentrevah as her leading man. It was true she had no script to work from so she would have to invent the dialogue ... that dialogue would of necessity include such words of affection as "darling." In the theater world the word was used gratuitously and she told herself it should be easy enough to drop a few darlings into the conversation without getting hot and bothered about it.

That was what she told herself and the very next instant was hiding her face in the pillows as stage fright shook her from head to heel.

She couldn't go through with it! She would have to back out! She'd dress, go down carrying her cases and firmly tell him that she was on her way to St. Mawgan.

HALF AN HOUR LATER Janie went downstairs dressed in a pleated skirt and leaf-green sweater, minus her suitcases and feeling ashamed of her own cowardice. Pagan Pentrevah was there in the hall leafing through some letters and the moment Janie set eyes on him she knew why she was playing his outrageous game of make-believe.

He fascinated her as equally as he frightened her and no man had ever done that to her before. He made her feel... reckless. Yes, that was how she felt, as if he had given her a wild wine to drink that had chased all the sober good sense out of her head.

He glanced up and studied her as she paused at the foot of the blackwood stairs, its treads and polished rails rising up around her in a kind of frame.

His eyes flicked her up and down. "Your 'companion's' wardrobe won't do," he said curtly. "You're going to need the kind of clothes that I'm expected to afford. The shops as St. Ives will provide them so we'll go there today—in my car!"

Instantly Janie was on the defensive. "You'll have a hopeless struggle trying to make me as glamorous as Roxanne. The objective, surely, is that you've taken an entirely different sort of wife?"

"Be that as it may—" he flung the letters back into

the salver "—I want you to be dressed convincingly. I'm not saying your clothes aren't good, it's just that they're too prim and proper, if what you're wearing is a sample of what you have in your luggage."

"Prim and proper!" A flash of temper lighted Janie's eyes. "What sort of a wife do you want me to be—a tart?"

They glared at each other, and then the spat was over as a smile came and went at the edge of his mouth. "You spark off when your tinder's touched, don't you? I'm merely suggesting that you be rigged out to suit your position as mistress of all this." He swept an expressive hand around the great hall. "No producer puts on a play without dressing his cast to suit the production, does he?"

"No," she admitted grudgingly. "But it never entered my head that you would want to provide a—a trousseau."

"Why?" His eyes held hers wickedly. "Because being provided with a trousseau makes the whole thing a little more real? It's a look of reality that I'm striving for."

"So long as it only *looks* real, Mr.—"

"Pagan!" he interrupted in a loud voice. "By hell, no wonder you're an out-of-work actress!"

"And no wonder you're a deserted husband," Janie shot back at him, her temper flaring right up as he touched her on a tender spot. It not only hurt but it made her anxious being without a part in a play. Even the repertory companies were cutting down on their output of plays and putting on those with a short cast list.

"I suppose I deserved that one," he said, and with a brief tilt of his head he acknowledged her riposte.

"If the edge on your appetite matches the one on your tongue, young woman, then you're in dire need of your breakfast. We go this way!"

She followed him and thought that he walked as a creature of the jungle walks, noiselessly and with the peculiar grace of big men, as if early on they developed a skill at being adept with their bodies rather than clumsy. He turned into a passageway, a slight swagger to the shoulders that tapered down into the disciplined waist and hips, his calf muscles pressing against the whipcord trousers.

A power emanated from him and made Janie clench her hands at her sides. He had in him a vital energy that she felt was drawn not only from the wild moorland and the sea but from emotions held in rein all the years he had been apart from the woman who, as a velvet-clad bride, had stood with him as the pagan fires leaped and glowed across Cornwall on the eve of their marriage.

That memory had burned him like a brand. Janie felt sure the pain of it never really left him in peace. He hated what he loved, the woman who had profaned his love, his house, his very name by an act he couldn't forgive.

Roxanne had destroyed the son that each Pentrevah hoped for so their links with the past and the future could remain unbroken. Perhaps from vanity she had killed what had certainly been a living human being after ten weeks in the womb. Janie's fingernails dug into the palms of her hands. He had every right to be angry, but would his desperate act of exorcism do the trick?

He paused in the doorway of the glassed-roof conservatory that he had called the flower room. And, indeed, when Janie entered the room she saw that plants and flowers were banked into pots and hanging baskets of all sizes. Upon a cane-plaited table with cane chairs at either side stood an array of covered dishes, the silver domes catching the sunlight that came through the glass roof.

"Be seated." He gestured at the table. "I often take breakfast here."

"It's very attractive, Mr.—"

"Pagan!" This time he didn't shout the name but said it with a kind of purring menace, and taking a stride he held out one of the chairs so she could sit down.

"Th-thank you—"

"Say my name, Jane. It isn't that difficult to pronounce."

She sat there, feeling him above her. "Don't rush me into everything," she breathed. "I feel as if I've been swept along by a gale as it is."

"Ah, perhaps so." He strode around to his own chair and sat down so he was directly facing her. "All the same, child, you have to accustom yourself to using my name. I grant that in certain of Jane Austen's novels the wives remain amusingly formal even after producing a batch of daughters, but I'd prefer a little less formality between you and I. Understood?"

Janie shook out her table napkin, perhaps to hide the fact that her hand was none too steady. Did she understand fully what he expected of her? Would she be this apprehensive if she felt this was a straightforward arrangement?

"You may pour the tea, Jane." He quizzed her across the table, a glint in his eyes that could have been wickedness, or the sun catching light in them.

She lifted the pot while he examined the contents of the dishes. The aroma of bacon and potato cake wafted to Janie and she felt her hungry insides react to the delicious smell. Potato cake, piping hot and buttery, and a dish of mushrooms.

"Will you take a helping of each, Jane?"

"Please!" Her reply was fervent, and as she pushed his cup and saucer across to him she caught the amused quirk to the edge of his lip.

"My cook is a Mrs. Pelham and she's the best there is in these parts." He piled food onto a plate for Janie. "I'll get her daughter to maid for you. I happen to know that she wants something grander than cleaning out the fireplaces and polishing the furniture."

"But I don't need a maid," Janie exclaimed.

"It's obligatory for the mistress of a house like mine. You might not have noticed just yet, my dear, but the Towers isn't exactly a semidetached on the outskirts of Wimbledon."

"I know that. I'm not a fool, but I just don't see the point of a maid. It isn't as if I'm in any real sense the mistress of your house."

"The point is, Jane, you have to appear to be and that makes the provision of a maid essential. Salt, pepper?" He pushed the cruet across to her, having just sprinkled his own breakfast with pepper.

Janie added a little salt to the side of her plate. "It's all very involved, and why are you going to all this trouble after all this time? Surely you're a match for any woman?" Janie chewed mushroom and flicked her eyes across his face. Any woman, she reflected, except one he might still love with the hot fires that time and pain and disillusion had not extinguished.

"Isn't there a saying," she murmured, "that God sends sinners a chance to repent? Perhaps Roxanne is coming back to Cornwall with that in mind?"

"She can repent all she damn well likes," he rejoined, and the edge of his lip seemed to snarl. "I don't happen to choose to forgive."

"Are you so proud and adamant, Mr.—Pagan?"

"Ah, at last you've managed to get your lips around my name! Yes, Jane, I'm proud and I hold hard the honor of this house. She'll not get a second chance to drag the Pentrevah name through the mud of a lot of gossip and scandal. Do you imagine there weren't other things I had to overlook while she lived here? Her flirtations with friends of mine! Her gluts of spending, and her quarrels with my staff! Her outrageous assumption that she was beauty and I was the beast who would condone the abortion of *my baby*! I'll see her in hell first!"

"Haven't you thought…." Janie jabbed at a piece of mushroom. "There's bound to be a lot of talk when people find out the truth—about us."

"There's been talk before. It will give them something else to prattle about." Suddenly his eyes narrowed and fixed upon Janie. "Worried about your reputation, is that it?"

"Yes." It was a lot easier than saying that she was worried about the intimate aspects of pretending to be the wife of this so out of the ordinary complex and compelling man. It was a pretense that would involve them in a very realistic kind of acting, and she didn't entirely trust him. He was deeper than anyone she had ever met before and she could feel him enticing her deeper into his scheme even as she struggled to pull herself out of it.

CHAPTER FIVE

"WHEN ALL THIS IS OVER and done with," a cryptic smile edged his mouth, "you'll be going back to London and that's a long way from Cornwall and any of the gossip that is likely to arise from your sojourn at the Towers."

"I-I don't think you care tuppence about my reputation." She was on the defensive as her eyes fenced with his. "You just want your own way and I'm supposed to let you have it. You must take me for a real little idiot!"

"On the contrary, Jane, I take you for a rather unusual sort of girl." He lifted the lid off the remaining mushrooms. "Will you share these with me? I picked them fresh myself, on my way across the moor to attend to your vehicle. That's a nice little Morgan you have. I take it you were going at quite a lick when your tire got punctured."

"I enjoy driving. That's part of my arrangement with Mrs. Burford."

"It was part of the arrangement, Jane." He said it casually. "More of these?"

"I've had sufficient, thank you." Her throat had gone dry and she poured herself some more tea. She was right about him, he was ruthless as a hawk in pursuit of his quarry and if she had an ounce of sense left in her she'd leap to her feet and dash headlong out of his house. Her car was now roadworthy and there was a lot of mileage in the dashing sports car she had bought secondhand.

"Women are rather like mushrooms." He held one speared on his fork. "Delicious and yet dangerous if you pick one at random; as a kiss that melts in the mouth or destroys like the death cap. I know what's going through your mind, Jane. You don't think you can trust me to be the perfect gentleman."

"Can I?" She regarded him across the rim of the cup in her hands then, dry throated, she gulped the tea.

"I can't really say, so at least I'm honest." His strong white teeth chewed the dark mushroom.

"According to Pinero," Janie spooned peach jam onto a triangle of toast, "there are these days no more rules to break, but you've found one, haven't you— Pagan?"

He smiled briefly as if the little stumble in her voice amused him. "A change of circumstances creates new rules, but I have to confess that I was never a man to bow down low to the conventions."

"Maybe that's why people said you and Roxanne were made for each other.... You both break the rules, don't you?"

"The ones I break, my child, aren't involved with the callous slaughter of the innocent. Do you think I can't see the innocence in your eyes? They're elusive, changing from calm to calamity like the sea off the rocks of Spanish Bay. The doubts are churning in your mind like the sea as it tosses itself at the rocks and fights to batter them down, but it takes many turns of the tide and many lashings of the waves to finally wear down a rock to sand grains."

"So I'm the water and you're the rock, is that it?"

"Isn't it?"

Her gaze flickered away from his disturbing eyes, but he went on looking at her, scrutinizing her hair that was styled pageboy, her mouth that was softly sticky and sweet from the peach jam, the wing-away slant to her brows above her changing eyes.

"Life is a game of chance, Jane, and if there hadn't been a chunk of rock on the road to St. Mawgan then you wouldn't be sitting here. Are you wishing like mad that you weren't sitting here—with me?"

She kept her gaze fixed on a hanging fuschia in a basket, the rose pink flowers dangling there like tiny dancers in midair. "You have to admit that your... scheme is an unorthodox one. I do feel as if I'm being sucked into something deep and I-I admit I'm scared."

"Scared of me, or that you'll bungle your part and perform unconvincingly as Mrs. Pagan Pentrevah?"

"I'm bound to," she said tensely. "I've had no practice at being a wife—real or unreal!"

"You've never played such a part onstage?"

"Not to date." She gave a slight shrug. "I usually play the artless ingenue."

"I'm unsurprised."

"You would be!" Her eyes flashed to meet his. "It's because you take me for an ingenuous little fool that you've managed to hook me by playing on my sympathy—and my need to earn some money."

"Perhaps there's an element of truth in what you say." His eyes teased the color into her cheeks. "Added to which you have a touch of class, something rather lacking in the gorgeous Roxanne! In her case breeding had run its course, but I was too smitten by her beauty to notice that she lacked grace of spirit. I learned the hard way, by hell!"

Never in her life had Janie heard such bitterness in

a voice, or seen such a range of emotions in a pair of eyes. She felt that a battle was raging inside Pagan as the old desires flared up and tried to overcome his longing to strike back at Roxanne for the way she had treated his love for her. He wanted so much to hate her because she had been less perfect than her face; he had thought he held an angel in his arms and discovered that she was vain and unscrupulous.

Maybe he could have forgiven her the vanity and self-love, but not the unnecessary aborting of his baby son.

"You didn't realize, eh, that offstage passions can be just as melodramatic as those played out in a theater?" He spoke with irony. "How you've managed to stay so innocent in such a profession is something of a mystery."

Janie had to admit to herself that it was a mystery when she thought of some of the emotional scrapes other girls in the profession got into. But those affairs now seemed innocuous when compared with the destructive forces let loose between Pagan Pentrevah and his wife. A shiver ran through Janie, as if a breath of wild moorland wind had found its way into the flower room.

He had severed himself by law from Roxanne, but Janie felt certain that his spirit was still tied to the woman with whom he had lived in this house so intimately, so passionately, finally with pain.

"Shall we shake on it?" His voice cut across her thoughts and she gazed hesitantly at the hand he held out to her across the table.

The wise course would be for her to refuse. But of its own accord her hand went out to him and as his strong fingers clasped hers, a kind of vibration ran upward into the pit of her arm, sending darts of sensation down into her rib cage where her heart beat so rapidly.

It was like a flame running along the edge of her bones.

"Oh, Lord," she breathed, "I'm going to need some chutzpah, aren't I?"

"Surely it takes a bit of cheek to walk out on a stage?" His eyes raked over her face, their dark centers glinting. "You have class and in some expensive clothes—"

"No." Her fingers wrenched free of his. "I don't want you spending money on clothes for me—I don't see the necessity for it. I-I think it's going a little too far, can't you see that?"

"Hmm, perhaps you're right." He leaned back in his chair and slid a cheroot between his lips, lighting it slowly so the smoke wreathed around his face and seemed to dissolve in the thought lines that creased his forehead.

"Yes, why buy a set of new clothes when there are closets bulging with them up in that damn room that I locked up years ago. I expect you could find at least a dozen outfits among that lot, and no doubt your grandmother taught you to sew if any of them need alterations."

"Roxanne's clothes?" Janie felt appalled by his suggestion, and yet she saw the logic in it. They had cost a lot of money and the fabrics were probably quite lovely... making do with those would eliminate the need for new ones, and Janie shrank irrationally from the idea of visiting a dress shop with him and seeing him write out a check in payment. Somehow it would make her feel... bought.

"You don't like the idea, Jane?" He quirked an eyebrow. "She was choosey about what she bought and they haven't been touched since the night she left me. The closets are of oak and no moths would have got in to spoil the silks and satins. Think of it as a theatrical wardrobe, and believe me in a sense it is. Roxanne used to change her outfits half a dozen times a day, acting out her various roles as mistress of the manor, Diana of the hunting field, and Aphrodite of the waves. In her closets she has just about everything.... Maybe I should have burned the lot."

"You couldn't," Janie said quietly. "Those garments had been next to her skin and it would have been like burning her."

"The total exorcism," he murmured. "That's why they burned witches in the old days. By hell, I insist that you do it, Jane! You'll wear her clothes and you'll come with me right now to have a look at them!"

Even as he spoke he rose from the table and came around to where Janie sat. He hoisted her to her feet and, holding her firmly by the elbow, he hurried her from the flower room, across the hall and up the stairs. His impetuosity took her breath away so that by the time they halted in front of a door she was panting and in no fit state to resist him. She watched him detach a small key from a watch chain, stride into the room, which proved to be a study lined with books, and unlock the top drawer of a big antique desk. He took a polished wood box from the drawer, unlocked that and took from it a much larger key. Janie also noticed that he withdrew some other object from the box and thrust it into a pocket of his whipcord trousers.

"Come, this way!" Again she was hurried into the galleried depths of the house and suddenly around a bend lighted by a huge oriel; in the glass were colored fleur-de-lis.

"Here we are!"

It was a house of tall doors to admit tall men, and Janie held her breath as he unlocked this door with the key that had been locked up in his desk. The unoiled door groaned as it was opened; the room beyond was drenched in shadow and stale air. Flicking on a wall light he went across to the windows and flung back the long velvet draperies that disgorged their dust and caused him to give a hefty sneeze.

"As you can see, Jane, this room hasn't been entered for years." He thrust open the windows to let in air and sunlight. Dust danced in the sun rays as Janie took a tentative step inside Roxanne's deserted bedroom. She stood just inside the door, nervously aware that in this room Pagan Pentrevah had slept with his real wife.

Overhead the painted ceiling was smirched with cobwebs and the patina of the furniture was cloudy with layers of dust and disuse. The sun through the dirty windows couldn't seem to shift the shadows that lurked in the corners of the room.

Janie gazed speechlessly across at the enormous bed that was entirely draped in a fur bedspread.

Erotic, Janie thought, sensuous and cruel. The sign of someone who had enjoyed power and used her body to exert it. Janie had a vivid mental image of a naked white body curled invitingly on the brown fur, limbs stretched out indolently.

"Well, Jane?" murmured the man who had possessed Roxanne on the fur. "What do you think?"

Janie couldn't have told him if he had offered her a ruby for her thoughts. She turned her gaze from the bed to the dressing table, which was an untidy jumble of cosmetic jars, perfume bottles, rouge pots and *dolls*. Victorian dolls in crinolines lolling among the pots and jars like miniature artistes of a long-closed music hall.

It was evident that not an article in this room had been touched or shifted since Roxanne's departure. Everything had been left just as it was the night she and Pagan had their terrible row. Janie's gaze followed a trail of spilled face powder across the carpet to a cheval glass on a drawer stand with carved posts at either side of the long mirror. She caught her breath as her reflection was thrown back at her, distorted by a crack that ran the length of the glass.

There on the floor lay the cut glass powder bowl that Roxanne had presumably thrown at her husband, missing him and cracking the mirror from top to bottom. The mirror now making distortions that added a menace to this disordered room where savage words had been flung back and forth.

"Say something, Jane."

When she met his eyes they were a raw sort of gold in his dark face.

"I-I don't know what to say." She gnawed her lip. "The room certainly needs a good cleaning out."

"I'll get Agatha to see about it."

Janie gave him an astonished look and he quirked an eyebrow. "You're the new mistress, aren't you? It's to be expected that you'd order this room to be rid of its cobwebs and its clutter—not to mention its ghosts."

"Are ghosts as easily swept away as cobwebs?" she asked.

He considered her question, his face looking hard and shadowed. "Maybe not. When your dreams go on the rocks—" He shrugged and bent to pick up a filmy stocking, which he held a moment and then flung aside again.

"When that happens, looking ahead seems as futile as a skipper of a damaged ship mapping the course for his journey ahead. I had made plans in which a son figured but it became evident I counted my chicks even as a vixen was slitting their throats."

The expressive words lingered in the room as he slowly glanced around him. "This particular room always fascinated Roxanne, that's why she wanted it for her own. There's a story that long ago a reluctant bride of the resident Pentrevah was locked in here alone on her wedding night. The husband was supposed to have said to her, 'We'll see which bridal you prefer, a lonely one or a loving one.' In the morning, according to the saga, she was found dead near the window and the reason for her death was never discovered. My theory is that the poor wretched girl poisoned herself.... She was said to be religious and had wanted to be a nun and she probably wore one of those rings with a poison concealed in it. Anyway, whether fact has been enlivened by fiction, this room does have an atmosphere. Do you sense it, Jane?"

"There's a drift of scent." Janie spoke the words almost cautiously, as if a shape unseen might be listening to her. "I think it's carnation scent."

"Is it?" He tensed his nostrils and breathed deeply. "It could be something of Roxanne's lingering in the room."

"No." Janie gestured at the dressing table. "The names on those labels are Chanel and Dior."

"They would be." His smile was brief and savage. "Nothing but the most expensive for Roxanne. And from the look of her that day I saw her in London I'd say she had found some other besotted fool to lavish on her whatever she wished for."

He stood there tall and dark, his eyes fixed broodingly upon the fur-draped bed. "Just take a look at that! My housekeeper was shocked to the bottom of her Cornish spine the day Roxanne put that on the bed for the first time."

Abruptly he strode to the bed and stripped off the cover, tossing it to the floor and giving the heap of fur a savage kick. Janie sensed from his behavior that her mental image of a naked figure on the fur had been a vivid one. She knew that Pagan was seeing that image in all its detail, Roxanne's eyes filled with witchery, her white limbs inviting his touch....

"You smell carnations, Jane," he murmured. "I smell only the warm flesh of a woman who didn't come as a timid or reluctant bride to this room. By hell, I'll have every inch of this damn den scrubbed out until the only scent left is that of carbolic. All that junk where she sat paying homage to herself can go in the garbage.... Those damn dolls, they look like a bunch of harlots!"

He came back toward Janie, holding out a hand. "Come, I can't ask you to wear anything that she wore. Let's go!"

"I-I'd like to see her things." Janie backed away before he could touch her. "May I?"

He frowned, then shrugged his shoulders. "Why not? Then I'll have a bonfire made of them."

He turned to the ceiling-high range of closets, oaken and carved in Tudor style. He flung open the doors and there was a shimmer of color, of shadow playing across silk, velvet and crepe de chine as he ran a large hand along the collection of gowns. "This lot she wore in the evenings, either here at the Towers or when we dined out. Morning, noon or night she had a gift for looking gorgeous and she knew it. There wasn't a man who ever saw her who didn't want to

have her. She reveled in it, dressed up to it, and looking like some exclusive tulip she would cling to my
arm 'when we entered a room or a restaurant and I'd
know that every man in that room was looking at her
and envying me. If she flirted with any one of them, I
was indulgent about it because—" He broke off and
stared at the dresses, his shoulders slumping as if the
weight of his memories was almost too much to bear.

"There was a time, Jane, when I never doubted her
love for me. A man has to be an almighty fool not to
know when a woman is faking her responses, but I
knew that Roxanne never put on any kind of act when
she was in my arms. We had—something, but she had
to go and destroy it. She cut most of it out of me, just
as she allowed some money-grubbing quack to cut my
son out of her. Even if I still loved her, I'd never stop
hating her for that. It was so needless, so damn heart-
less—with her looks and my strength, what a boy he
would have been!"

It was a cry straight from the depths of him, and
Janie felt certain that never again in her life would she
feel anything like the cold, cold thrill that coursed
through her when she heard his *cri de coeur.*

Janie felt like an intruder. He couldn't seriously
have intended that she make a pretense of stepping
into Roxanne's high-heeled shoes. The cheval glass
gave back Janie's reflection, cracked and odd; people
would smile cruelly if she walked into a room holding
onto his arm!

"You wanted to see these." His voice cut across
her thoughts as jaggedly as the glass cut her image.
"Well, here they are." A heap of dresses landed on
the oaken stool at the foot of the bed, a sprawl of fine
fabrics and breathtaking colors. The beautiful dense
mauve of tulips caught Janie's eye and she saw a fig-

ure swaying slightly on dagger-heels, fingers clenching a dark-clad arm, the mauve silk clinging to every
rich curve of a body that made men wet their lips.

"You're right," Janie said tensely, "I couldn't wear
her clothes, or make out that I'm the second Mrs. Pentrevah. Let's call it off and let me be on my way—"

"You aren't backing out on me!" His hands
gripped her until she felt painfully sure he'd leave his
fingerprints in her flesh. His eyes blazed down at her.
"It was your idea to poke your nose into her closets
and now you've seen the kind of things she used to
wear, you've got the feel of the kind of woman she
was. I warned you she was unusually beautiful, but
that doesn't mean that you aren't attractive. I'm set
on going through with this scheme of mine."

"No one's going to believe that you'd marry me
after being married to Roxanne. If this was for real
and not just a game, you'd admit it yourself. Go on,
admit it."

He stared down at her, then with his great strength
Pagan lifted her clear off her feet and the next instant
he crushed her lips with his and almost stopped her
breath in her throat.

"Marry me for real, Jane."

The incredulous words whirled through her mind.
The next instant she went limp, and the following instant became dazedly aware that he had lain her on
the bed and was gently but firmly slapping her cheek.

"Fool girl," his voice came from a distance. "What
is there to faint about?"

"I-I wouldn't marry you," she said faintly, "if you
were the last man left in England."

"That's flattering, I must say!"

"You're married," Janie struggled to sit up, "married in your heart to Roxanne, forever and ever."

"Jane, for God's sake don't say that to me!" The next moment he was bearing her back on the bed, an avalanche of angry power and muscle.

"No!" she cried out.

"No? The little wife is saying no already?" The voice was a woman's and it came from the doorway. Pagan sat up as if electrified, thrusting the disordered black hair out of his eyes as he turned his head toward the figure standing in the aperture of the door.

"You!" Janie heard him exclaim.

"Yes." The woman stood there just beyond the sunlight streaked with dust and softly laughed.

CHAPTER SIX

"I CAN SEE you weren't expecting company, brother mine. Agatha's just informed me that you've sprung a surprise and married a girl from London, of all places."

At these words Janie nearly fainted again. She lay there dumbly as Pagan slid off the bed and straightened to his full height, whose impressiveness somehow diluted the indignity of being caught, sprawled upon Janie, by his sister.

Janie wanted desperately to refute what his sister had said about their being married, but her vocal chords had somehow developed a blockage and this gave Pagan the chance he wanted. Quite deliberately he committed her to his lie.

"Tristana, come and meet your new sister-in-law. Her name is Jane, and the little tussle you witnessed just now was over this." From his pocket he took a small box and pressed the spring. Something glittered and the next instant he had taken firm hold of Janie's left hand and pushed onto her third finger a ring such as she had never seen in her life before.

She could only gaze speechlessly at the sheer beauty of the diamond held in gold claws, glowing and alive, with a deep blue flame licking at the heart of it.

The brilliance of the stone was in her eyes when she raised them to Pagan, but even dazzled she wasn't quite blinded to the raw look of entreaty that sprang into his eyes.

"Jane is one of those girls," he said, "who believes in giving rather than taking, but she'll wear the ring now it's on her finger. You're witness to that, eh, Tris?"

His sister strolled to the foot of the bed. She was tall like her brother, dark like him, striking to look at, with a small crescent scar embedded in the tanned skin of her face. The resemblance to Pagan was there but her eyes were different, they were a deep honey brown and the look in them was amazed as she scrutinized Janie from her tousled hair down slowly to her size-four shoes.

"Ye gods!" Tristana exclaimed. "This time you've been robbing the cradle, haven't you? So this is what you had up your sleeve, a child bride."

"I'll admit there's a difference in our ages," he rejoined, "but Jane is hardly a child."

"Is Jane aware that this is your second trip to the altar?" Tristana shifted her gaze to her brother. "Was it an altar, by the way?"

"Registry office." He didn't bat an eyelid. "No fuss nor frills, that's why I wanted to compensate Jane with a nice ring."

"Nice?" Tristana gave a scoffing laugh. "That's the understatement of the year. You've given her one of the family heirlooms...the ring you promised Roxanne when she had the—"

Tristana broke off as a frown darkened her brother's face. "Sorry, but this has come as a bit of a shock. She doesn't say much, does she?"

"You'd be surprised," he drawled. "Come along, Jane, say something or Tris will think I've married a dumb blonde."

"How do you do?" Janie said obediently. Inwardly she was furious with him for trapping her into deceiving his sister. Furious and at the same time aware of the tension in him, as if he'd clap a hand over her mouth if she denied that they were married.

"I'm fine, thanks." Tristana studied Janie curiously. "Are you shy, or plain scared of Pagan? You'll have to snap out of it or he'll chew you up and spit out the pieces."

"I doubt that," he smiled. "Jane's too tender to be indigestible."

"You do sound smitten." Tristana gave him a curious look. "It must have been love at first sight."

"It was," he agreed.

"On both sides?"

"Jane is here to prove it, isn't she?"

Once again Tristana swept her eyes over Janie. "Do you ride?"

"I was brought up on a farm and had a pony when I was five."

"I see. You met Pagan in London, didn't you?"

"I work in London. I'm on the stage."

"You're kidding me!"

"I'm telling the truth." Janie put a lot of feeling into the word.

"Don't tell me you were in the chorus?" Tristana looked at her brother and gave a laugh. "I can't picture Pagan as a backstage Johnny, no more than I can imagine a girl like you kicking her legs up in the air."

"I'm a straight actress." Janie wasn't quite sure if she was going to like Pagan's sister; she certainly wasn't making much of an effort to be friendly. She seemed intent on the reverse.

"How did the two of you come to meet?"

The question had been inevitable and Janie left Pagan to supply the answer.

"Quite by chance," he said casually. "Jane's car—

it's an attractive little Morgan—was acting temperamental so I came to her rescue. We got talking, you know how it is."

"Two lonely people," his sister drawled, "with little else to do but...fall in love?"

"Exactly." He cast a glance at Janie which she took to mean was her cue to join him in their pas de deux.

"I suppose you could call it...fate," she said, rather inaudibly.

"What happens about your stage career?" Tristana asked. "This part of Cornwall isn't exactly the center of things theatrical, though it's true we do have our little dramas. There won't be much opportunity for you to do any acting."

The irony of the remark drew Janie perilously close to blurting out that she was acting right now, playing a role that petrified her with its dishonesty and its pitfalls.

It was her turn to look at Pagan with entreaty in her eyes.

"Jane will find sufficient outlet for her dramatic skills in being my wife," he said smoothly. "From now on she'll be the mistress of the manor and will have to act the part."

"Is that what he said to you, Jane?" His sister looked mocking. "Will you take on the job of acting to the manor born? I mean, you being an actress and all that?"

Janie's heart thumped. "Something like that."

"Don't mind me saying so, but you look a bit scared, as if afraid you've put your head on the block and it could get sliced off."

Perhaps in a sense that was what was happening to her. Her body did feel as if it was adrift from her mind, which until Pagan Pentrevah's advent into her

life had never led her this far astray from rational behavior. She had always congratulated herself upon
being levelheaded; a girl who had set her sights on a
successful stage career, with no traumatic romances to
mess up her life.

"Anyway—" Tristana glanced around the big dusty
bedroom "—what are the pair of you doing smooch-
ing in this room? It's been locked up for years....
Don't tell me you're going to make use of it?"

"I felt that Jane had the right to see all the house,"
Pagan replied. "I agree with her that the room needs
cleaning and clearing out."

"What, are you going to clear these out?" Tristana
walked over to the dress closets and ran a hand along
the garments, then she glanced at the ones strewing
the oak stool. "Does Jane know about—"

"Yes," he broke in. "Jane has been told that this
room belonged to my former wife Roxanne. She
knows all the relevant details."

"Does she?" Tristana gave him an intent look,
then she shrugged slightly. She moved her gaze to
Janie. "What do you think of all these? They must
have cost the earth. Good Lord, I never realized Roxy
had so many things! I was only a kid when she was
living here and more interested in my ponies and getting down to the seashore. I realized that she always
looked stunning—Pagan has told you that she was
probably the most beautiful creature from Land's
End to John O'Groats?"

"Yes, I've been told all about her." Janie slid off
Roxanne's bed as she spoke and moved away from
it, stroking creases from her skirt and sliding a hand
over her hair. On her left hand she could feel the
weight of the Pentrevah diamond...the ring that he
had planned to give Roxanne. Janie wanted to wrench

it off her finger, but she would have to restrain herself until she was alone with Pagan. Perhaps she could convince him that the ring should be relocked in his desk, along with the key to this memory-haunted room.

Tristana took hold of one of the long dresses and held it to her nose a moment. "I smell perfume," she said. "Only it's different from what's on this dress. It's a garden flower scent, probably yours, Jane."

"It's like carnations," Janie replied, "but I use Givenchy's L'interdit."

"Mine's usually horse," Tristana smiled. "Intriguing, wouldn't you say? And you're right, it is a smell of carnations.... Have we a ghost, do you think? Cornwall's riddled with them but I've never sensed one in this house before. You've probably encouraged it, Pagan, by keeping this bedroom locked up like Bluebeard's chamber."

"Whatever the damn smell is," he chided her, "keep your voice down, Tris. You know what Mrs. Pelham is like and I don't want to lose her; she makes the best squab pie this side of the Tamar, not to mention her sand screws."

"Aren't men romantic?" Tristana shook her head at him. "Your love of pilchards apart, brother, you aren't really serious about dumping all these beautiful things, are you? Look at this, for instance." She took from the closet near at hand an evening dress in midnight black, patterned across the skirt with jewel-green leaves. "I'm not averse to looking glamorous in this when Hunt comes over from New York; you know what he said the last time he was here, that I was giving dresses a bad name. I hate all that business of shopping for the darn things and I feel at home in breeches, but I'd like to show him that I do have a figure to show off, and just look at the label on this dress! When were you in Paris?"

"On our honeymoon," he said curtly. "You were away at school."

"Oh, yes, I came home for the wedding, didn't I? And that evening we watched the midsummer fires being lighted across country and there was an enormous outdoor party."

Tristana moved her gaze slowly to Janie. "What a difference this time; it's all been very hush-hush, I must say. Poor Jane, most girls want a white-lace gown, organ music and the Lohengrin wedding march. Those words, 'to love, honor and cherish,' always sound more possible in a church, but of course they're only words, aren't they? It's intentions that count."

Janie just didn't know what to say, so she stood there silently. Let Pagan embroider the lies; she wasn't going to.

"Do you say those words in a registry office?" Tristana persisted, her eyes flicking the style of Janie's hair, its fairness caught in a ray of sunlight through the dust-speckled mullions.

"It's rather more formal," it was Pagan who answered her question, "and if you're set on some plunder, like some of our celebrated forebears, then by all means take what you fancy. This room is definitely due for a spring-cleaning."

"What about you, Jane?" His sister was still watching Janie with an inquisitive gleam in her eyes. "Do you like any of these things? What about this, for instance?" The dress she drew forth was of stunning ivory velvet, and pinned to it was a velvet cap sewn with pearls, a wilted bunch of orchids, and a blue garter.

Janie stared at the dress and felt a crawling of her

nerves. Tristana was putting her through some kind of a test and Janie knew she had to do one of two things, pass it or run very fast out of this room. Then as she hesitated she felt Pagan slide his arm around her waist and pull her unnervingly close to his hard body. He welded her there, his fingers pressed into her much tenderer flesh, sending a warning signal into her very bones.

"I shall be making a bonfire of that damn thing," he said gratingly.

"Seems a shame." Tristana looked straight at him. "Roxie wore a pearl cross with it. I remember how it gleamed against the velvet. Some of the people in church were a bit shocked that she chose orchids for her bouquet.... Tipped with flame, weren't they?"

"Whatever you're trying, Tris, it won't work. Jane knows all about the heaven and hell I had with Roxanne."

"A bowl of bitter cherries," his sister murmured. "Hoping for sweeter things with Jane?"

"Would she be here if I weren't?"

"I don't know, Pagan. There've been so many conflicting stories, haven't there?"

"Such as?"

"That you did away with Roxie in a fury of love-hate. That you've gone all these years without a woman because you can't forget her."

"They're just stories, little sister." A raffish smile was on the edge of his lips as he brushed them across the top of Janie's head. "I never did away with Roxanne, and as you can see I have a woman now." Tristana studied him with Janie, and never had Janie felt such stage fright as she felt right now; her audience of one was a girl not much older than herself but she could see suspicion in Tristana's eyes mixed with a tinge of antagonism. Pagan's sister didn't like it that her brother had supposedly married in secret. She was out to give him a hard time because, as she saw it, he had betrayed her trust in him—her right to be consulted when it came to bringing an addition into the Pentrevah family.

"There's another story," she said, a trifle insolently. "One I heard from Plum who got it from her mother.... That Roxie was brought from Ireland to live with her cousins because her mother died in an asylum when Roxie was eighteen months old. If it's true, then no wonder she—well, she obviously had good reason for being afraid that she'd pass on whatever it was that sent her mother out of her mind. These things are hereditary aren't they?"

There was silence, stillness, and then Janie felt Pagan withdraw his arm from around her waist and move bodily away from her. "When the hell did you hear this nonsense?" he demanded of Tristana. "It is nonsense. Servant-hall talk! Roxanne's mother died from a hunting fall; she broke her neck when her mount stalled at a jump and threw her."

"That's the embroidery." Tristana stood facing him, drawn up as he was to her full height, defying his eyes and their hawkish danger. "The plain truth is that she was mad and broke her neck falling down a flight of stairs at the asylum. Go and ask Mrs. Pelham! She evidently got the facts from the O'Hares's cook. Something about a letter that was read—on accident or purpose."

"I don't believe it!" He spoke the words in a low voice, a pained voice, as if he didn't want to believe it. "I'd have heard about this long ago. Roxanne and I were too close for such concealment. I'd be the first to know—"

"The last!" Tristana flung at him. "The O'Hares were desperate to keep it quiet, especially when it became obvious that *you* were going to marry Roxie. You're Pentrevah of the Towers and it was never a secret that you'd want a son to carry on the name. It's one of the Cornish legends, isn't it, that there has always been a direct heir to the name, the lands and the house? Roxie was well aware that her first duty lay in providing the son to carry on the Pentrevah tradition, but when she became pregnant she just couldn't go through with it, knowing what she knew—that there were seeds of madness in her."

"It's all a damn fabrication!" he roared, throwing out a hand toward the cheval glass with its jagged crack all the way down to the drawered base. "There was only one thing that really mattered to her and that was her own image—dressed to kill, dressed to conquer, and it tore her vanity to shreds when she saw herself getting out of shape. She couldn't endure the slight alteration that ten weeks made, it would have sent her crazy to go the whole nine months with her body distorted, as she saw it. I know!"

He flung the word at the mirror and stared into it as if he saw Roxanne reflected there, jaggedly. "I lived with her. I loved her. I was never blind to what she was—goddamned Salome born out of the loins of Sodom and Gomorrah! I accepted what she was. It didn't matter to me as long as I had her. I wanted her to be the mother of my son, but she killed him and there was murderous intent in me that night I found out. Maybe that's why she left me. Maybe I would have done her in had she stayed here, flaunting her flat stomach and her high breasts that no child was ever going to pull out of shape with its greedy little mouth—"

Suddenly with a groan Pagan was striding blindly to the door, pushing Tristana aside as he went. "Someone at the O'Hares has been lying about her mother. They'd want to paint me black, wouldn't they, after seeing her as the mistress here and then seeing it all at an end? They were the ones who went to the police with accusations about me—mighty foundless accusations as it happens!"

He stood there a moment in the doorway and his gaze flicked almost blindly over Janie, seeing her as if through a mist. "Roxanne has risen from the dead, little sister. Anyday now she'll be back in this part of the world, and there'll be a few red faces around. She hasn't been lying at the bottom of Prowler's Pool all these years.... She's been lying in some other man's downy bed!"

He was gone with the words, leaving a thunderous silence behind him. *Oh, God*, Janie thought, *I've got to get out of this house—now!*

"You look white as chalk!"

Janie glanced at Pagan's sister and was preparing to blurt out that she was no such thing as the second wife of Pentrevah, when Tristana came up to her and gripped her by the shoulder.

"I'm sorry to have been such a beast to you," she said, "but it came as such a shock...coming home from Helston where I've been staying with a friend to find that my brother has gone and married a total stranger to me. I knew there was *someone* but he might have confided in me. I am his sister and I care about him."

Tristana scanned Janie's face. "Are you terribly in love with him?"

Janie flinched, as if from hot metal.

"Sorry to be personal, but you don't look the sort,

somehow, to marry a man unless you cared a hell of a lot. I know that money and position are a consideration for some, but somehow you look—genuine."

Janie felt as genuine as a brass halfpenny, yet even though the true facts clamored at her lips for utterance, something held her back on the very brink of revealing them. In her mind she saw Pagan Pentrevah's harrowed face, heard again the raw note of torment in his voice when he spoke of Roxanne returning to bedevil him all over again.

"Is that story about Roxanne's mother a genuine one?" she found herself asking Tristana.

"I believe so." His sister looked worried. "I shouldn't have blurted it out the way I did, but I was up on my high horse over this marriage he's rushed into—" Tristana bit her lip. "You know what I mean, it has been rather sudden."

"Yes." Janie's gaze was abstracted. She was by nature someone who was quick to extend a helping hand to anyone in troubled waters, but she sensed a welter of trouble in the man who had just stormed out of the room. She was torn between getting out of his house before she got hurt herself and letting him cling to her hand. She had never faced such a dilemma, and then his sister resolved it for her.

"I can see why Pagan needs you, Jane. He can be a difficult man, but there are also times when he can be...how do I put it? Hard to resist?"

Janie sighed inwardly. If she left now she would never know the outcome of all this, but if she stayed she'd be taking the biggest risk of her life where Pagan Pentrevah was concerned.

Trouble and danger were incised into his dark features. He had the fascination of a panther pacing its cage, hungering to be free of what held him captive.

Janie couldn't help but wonder—perhaps hope—that she held the key that might set him free. It was a possibility that she found hard to resist.

"Shall we get away from this dusty morgue of a room and go and have some coffee?" Tristana flung aside the black-velvet dress she had been holding. "My throat is parched; how's yours?"

"Parched," Janie agreed. "Coffee would be a blessing."

At the bedroom door Janie glanced back a moment and saw her reflection in the cracked mirror. She looked as unreal as she felt. Then with a shiver she closed the door and followed Pagan's sister downstairs.

"Are you a good actress?" Tristana led Janie into a room with glass doors opening onto a terrace. Below the terrace, a rambling garden was ablaze with all sorts of shrubs and trees and low-built walls over which plants had grown in mats of gold and purple. The vista was an attractive one and Janie leaned on the terrace wall and took several deep breaths of the tangy air with moorland in it.

"I've been told I'm a good actress," she replied. "I love it."

"Yet you've gone and hitched your star to a Cornishman." Tristana sat down in a cane chair and crossed her long legs in boots and breeches "He isn't the sort of man to want a working wife, you do realize that?"

What Janie realized was that she had let it be thought that she really had married Pagan Pentrevah. She was enmeshed now in his web of intrigue and she had to act the part. She might even manage to live with the guilt she felt if she looked upon the whole thing as a play in which she played the leading lady.

"I have to admit," she said, "that I haven't yet

come to terms with the man who has put this ring on my hand. He's gone and swept me off my feet and I-I haven't yet come down to earth."

"You're so different in every way from Roxie that it's unbelievable.... You don't mind that I mention her, do you, Jane?"

"She's part of the history of this house, isn't she?" Janie gazed around her and felt in awe of this great house built of Cornish stone with its windswept walls and towers. The place and its people at one with the lonesome moors, the adamantine rocks and such strange trees as the dracaena. Beyond the terrace she could see great swaths of buttergold gorse, while overhead a falconlike bird etched itself in sculptured flight against the sky.

"We call them bee hawks." Tristana's gaze was intent upon Janie there by the terrace wall, looking somehow fragile in contrast to the graystone strength of the house and the wild moor that cradled it.

Janie watched the bee hawk out of sight, beyond the crags and tors of this legendary land that gave birth to powerful emotions that could hurt and haunt the people who felt them.

"The hawk is disdainful of easy prey, did you know that?" Tristana stroked a finger against the scar in her cheek. "He devours every scrap of what he catches, except for the feathers, which he scatters in the wind."

Janie looked across at Pagan's sister. "Do you think I've been easy prey for your brother?"

Tristana shrugged. "There's an animalism in some men that attracts the shyest of women, as well as the boldest."

An image of Pagan Pentrevah stole into Janie's mind. The way he moved with the easy control of a mettlesome animal, the pride and irony stamped into his features, his eyes that were ebony on gold.

"Sweet, kind, innocent girls get hurt, Jane, so watch your step."

"Who is going to hurt me?" Janie asked, even though she knew the answer.

"Who is it who hurts us the most?"

"The person closest to us."

"Exactly."

"You don't have to warn me," Janie said, getting into the part she had taken on. "I'm perfectly aware that your brother has never forgotten a hair or a curve of Roxanne, not a caress or a curse."

"Then you must care a great deal for him if you can accept all that."

"Sometimes we feel compelled to take on something that deep down gives us the jitters," Janie said with complete honesty.

"You have to be the martyr type to do that. Is that what you are, Jane?"

"I could have a yen to play Joan of Arc." Janie's smile was a little wry, for it was a role she longed to play onstage.

"She burned in the fires of conspiracy and a dash of religious mania, but I suppose love could be called a fire that burns in the heart. My brother's a very deep man, very Cornish."

"Like Prowler's Pool," Janie murmured.

"So you know about the bog, and about the bracelet? Roxie just went, taking nothing else but the bracelet, and it really did look as if she had either gone into the bog of her own accord, or been thrown into it. Pagan used to take part in Cornish hurling matches so it wouldn't put much strain on him to hurl a woman into a feather-bed bog, and the one on Pentrevah land is known to be fearfully deep. It has swallowed moor ponies...."

Janie felt a shiver run cold down her spine. "You could believe that of your own brother?"

"The passions of the Pentrevahs aren't milk and water, Jane. Haven't you found that out yet?" Tristana slid her eyes up and down Janie's slim body. "Don't tell me the honeymoon hasn't started yet?"

"You're being personal." It was absurd but Janie felt the heat of embarrassment sweep over her, as if she were really a coy bride who hadn't yet been bedded by her bridegroom.

"You're blushing so that answers my question. Ye gods, you've taken on a handful! Roxie could manage him but I don't see you doing it. She was a match for him in every way."

"She didn't manage to keep him," Janie retaliated. "She went a step too far and nearly had her neck broken by him."

"She did what had to be done. If your mother had died mad, would you want a baby?"

"It isn't always a fact that people go mad because it's in the blood. Things that happen in our lives can send us that way. I think Roxanne was ambitious, selfish, and too sure of herself."

"You're bound to be jealous of her," Tristana gibed. "You haven't her looks or her charisma. She could charm the birds out of the trees and one evening she proved it by imitating the song of a nightingale, which sang straight back at her, completely fooled. She was full of amusing tricks."

"I bet she was!" Janie had a cynical vision of a fur-covered bed. "If she was so clever, then why on earth did she tell Pagan she'd had an abortion? She could have pretended to have a miscarriage if she really feared for the child's mentality.''

Tristana had no answer, so Janie went on.

"It was because in her arrogance she believed she could get away with anything. She must have thought that Pagan's love for her was bottomless, but love in fact is a self-centered emotion and a part of us can't bear to have shattered the ideal image that we set up on that reserved shelf in the heart. We might go on caring for the shattered object but we know that the pieces can't be put back together without blemish.''

"So you'll live with Pagan knowing that someone else is still there in his heart, blemished or not?"

"I'll be honest with you," Janie said quietly. "Your brother needed me and that's why I'm here, but I have no deep trust in love. I knew a young, eager actress who fell for a man older than herself. He was already married and he spun her all the usual yarns about not being happy with his wife, who was supposedly a cold self-centered woman who didn't put herself out to make him happy.''

"My friend Penny believed everything he told her and she became devoted to him. We were both in the cast of *The Ritz at Noon* and this man would phone her in the evening, when she was offstage for half an hour. Then gradually his calls and their meetings grew less and he began to make threadbare excuses about being tied up by business problems. She grew sad and abstracted and would break into tears when she went offstage and there was no phone call for her, and no flowers in the dressing room I shared with her. She really cared for him, but all he wanted from her was the fun of conquest. Penny couldn't see that he wasn't worth a single teardrop let alone buckets of them. She wouldn't believe he was having her on a piece of string and dangling her over heartbreak cliff."

"One evening she didn't show up for the performance and another actress had to take over for her.... At the finale of the play, at curtain fall, we were told that Penny had swallowed half a pint of some awful fluid that people put down their drains to clear them— She died in hospital, her insides burned out, and somewhere that selfish swine she loved is driving around in his car and not caring a damn that a sweet kid killed herself because of him."

"That's a very sad story, Jane."

"It's a true one."

"It's frightening to think of caring that much for a man." Tristana shuddered. "No man is worth killing yourself over, and women can usually cry these things out of their systems. Perhaps your friend was the hysterical type."

"No," Janie shook her head. "She was a romantic."

"Maybe just as bad," Tristana mused. "It's rather got us by the throat that we all need to be loved, hasn't it?"

Janie made no answer, but unaware her hand went to her throat as if to protect it.

"I sometimes think about being loved," Tristana said, "in a devastating, greedy, totally protective way. Most women want that, so it must be awful to fall for someone who is really shallow, who only paddles around in the rock pools rather than the sea. That was what your friend Penny came up against. She couldn't live with the disappointment, but it was a drastic way to end things. A martyrdom!"

"Yes," Janie agreed.

"I hope—"

Janie stared at Tristana.

"You've gone and let yourself in for trouble, haven't you, especially if Roxanne is coming back to Cornwall." A frown creased Tristana's forehead. "Ye gods, is that why he married you?"

"You could say—that's why I'm here."

"Ye gods!"

CHAPTER SEVEN

THE HARDEST PART, as Janie knew well, was when the curtain rose and a performer stepped from the wings onto the stage and spoke her opening lines. It was then that a rapport was established with the audience if a performer was lucky.

Janie's moment came when she sat down that evening at the dining table in the big room with the hand-painted Chinese wallpaper, the immense oriental rug that covered most of the floor, the handsome rose-wood side-table, and the intricately carved chairs set around the table where a mound of bright red flowers was arranged in the center directly beneath a glittering great jewel of a chandelier.

It was like a stage setting and Janie strove to believe that she was taking part in a play and that the other people seated at the table were performers as well. One of them, at least, was putting on an act and that made it a little easier for Janie.

He looked big and masterful in his evening wear, and when he smiled across the silver and the cut glass that possessive gleam in his eyes was a brilliant piece of acting. "Pick up your wine glass, darling," he said. "We must drink a toast to each other."

"And then hurl the glasses into the fire?" The riposte sprang of its own accord to her lips, for it was exactly the kind of line this melodrama called for.

"It would seem the appropriate gesture," he

drawled, "except that these wineglasses are a hundred years old."

She watched his fingers as they toyed with the curved bowl and fragile stem of his own glass. Hands that had power and a certain ruthless attraction, the kind that might easily kill, or caress.

"To love." He raised his glass. "The most foolish of human follies yet life would be death without it."

"To love." Tristana was looking directly at Janie, waiting for her to echo the sentiment.

Janie lifted her glass and could feel the nervous weakness in her wrist as her fingers enclosed the stem. She mustn't drop the glass and break it; it was real and not a stage prop made of cheap plastic. It was real as the smell of the red flowers, the tinkle of the chandelier as a draft swung the pendants, the dryness in her throat.

"To the most foolish of human follies," she said, and felt a tiny sense of victory as she put her glass to her lips and took a deep swallow of the wine. It had a golden warmth and by the time she'd had a second glass of it she was no longer on edge with nerves. She ate and drank, and if she wasn't exactly merry, she at least managed to get through the evening in a pleasant haze.

But what a relief it was when at last she found herself alone in her room, even though it was connected to an adjoining room by a door without a key in the lock.

Her gaze dwelt reflectively on the pair of armchairs, one by the bed and the other by the window. It flitted through her mind that she would feel safer if one of the chairs was against the door. She almost suited the action to the thought, then decided that if Pagan Pentrevah was going to enter this room an armchair wouldn't keep him out; one thrust of one of those large hands and he'd be in here.

Janie, she chided herself, *you're behaving like a mid-Victorian spinster with the jitters!* Pagan Pentrevah was a gentleman even if he did resemble a pirate from the Spanish Main. Added to which, he was still violently attracted to Roxanne...that was why he regarded love as a folly. Why he was determined not to let the madly beautiful Roxanne make a fool of him again.

Almost unaware Janie found herself gazing into the shield mirror on the chest of drawers. It reflected back to her a pensive pair of eyes beneath a trim cap of hair. Her dress was along simple lines with a neat collar. The only exotic item about her was the diamond ring on her left hand. She studied the diamond, which was celestial in its bed of gold. She traced a fingertip over its facets, which were so brilliant they looked as if they might burn her finger.

A fake wife should have a ring of paste, she thought, and once again her eyes were upon the door that connected this large comfortable room with the one in which Pagan had his bed. A tremor shook Janie's knees. Gentleman or not, he was still the most masculine male Janie had ever encountered and if he chose to forget that she was only a wife on hire, there would be little she could do to protect herself against him.

Shaking her head as if to rid it of such thoughts Janie proceeded to get ready for bed. Her nightwear lay ready on the bed and she took it with her into the bathroom, which, like her bedroom, was old-fashioned in style but provided every kind of comfort. She undressed, took a shower and brushed her teeth. Towelling her hair, which dried pretty quickly, she dressed and wandered back into the bedroom.

It was the slippered feet she saw first, there between the windows where long velvet curtains draped the floor. She flung back the towel from her face and gazed at the tall robed figure with unveiled alarm in her eyes.

"Yes," he drawled, "they do change color according to your moods, don't they? Green chartreuse at this precise moment, with a dash of bitters."

"You—you shouldn't be in here!" she gasped.

"It's my house, Jane."

"I'm not yours!"

"You imagine that's why I'm in here, about to claim husbandly rights?"

She flushed and could feel her bare toes curling into the wool of the carpet. "What do you want? We said good night—"

"In front of my sister. We need to clarify a few details so do stop looking at me as if I've just stormed ashore from some pirate galleon and am about to tear off your pajamas and have my wicked way with you."

He said it mockingly, with an amused glint in his eye, but the trouble was that he looked dangerous as he stood there against the backdrop of peach curtains. In the dark opening of his robe his chest was bare and brown; his entire body was taut and spare with not an ounce of surplus weight on him.

He was vital as a javelin in a ruthless hand, Janie thought, and she was his target.

"Can't we talk in the morning? I-I'm tired."

"In the morning you can lie in bed until noon if you've a wish to do so. It will be accepted as perfectly natural."

Janie stared at him, feeling the nervous beat of her heart as the implication in his words struck home to her.

"Quite so," he drawled. "It's part of the arrangement that I should appear to pay you the usual attentions of a man with a new young wife. No one is going to believe that I'd do otherwise, Jane, so I'm here to tell you that each morning I plan to come in here and join you in bed—"

"No!" Her eyes blazed at him indignantly. "I'm not having that!"

"You have little choice my dear." He said it lazily and strolled to the four-poster, which he surveyed from the canopy to the lace-edged pillows, plump and white where the sheets lay open in readiness for Janie to climb in.

"It's certainly large enough for two,"

"You're playing games with me—"

"No, Jane." He swung around to face her, his hands thrust into the pockets of his robe. "You've agreed to conspire with me to make it look as if I'm well and truly married to you. Servants talk and I want it all around the locality that I have me a young bride and I'm busy bedding her. If I'm seen in your bed in the mornings and we take breakfast together, then the natural assumption will be that I've spent the entire night in your charming company. I thought I'd let you know the procedure in order to have you rehearsed in your mind for the morning."

He paused and his black brows gabled his eyes. "For heaven's sake, child, do you have to look as if what I'm suggesting is the height of indecency? I'm merely going to come in here, discard my robe, and slip into that bed at your side. Then I shall ring for breakfast and the scene will be set for some juicy gossip in the kitchen."

"I won't do it!" Janie defied him, her damp hair tousled above her defiant eyes. "If you expected me to go that far, then you're barking up the wrong tree! It isn't right—"

"By hell!" He took an angry step toward her. "Don't be such a damn little prig! I don't intend to lay my rough hands on your precious little body...as if I'd want to." His eyes stripped her, from her neck to her bare feet. "In those pajamas you look about as seductive as a scrag end of mutton, so consider yourself entirely safe from my baser impulses, if that's why you're shaking at the knees."

"I'm not."

"You're a liar as well as a prig," he taunted her. "Hasn't any man given you a thorough good kissing yet? It's probably what you need.... Who was it said that men had better watch out for the puritanical virgin who hides her fire beneath a layer of ice?"

"He sounds a fool whoever he was," she retorted. "Fire and ice could only produce a nice big puddle of water. I hope I'm not that wet!"

"Just a little damp around the edges." Pagan's eyes slid more slowly over Janie. "Haven't you had the usual crush yet on an older man? You're the type for it, aren't you? Father ran out on your mother when you were a tot, so you grew up with your grandparents and when the time came for you to choose a career you chose the fantasy world of the theater, with its make-believe people living invented lives. You're a dreamer, Jane."

"I know I am," she admitted. "It isn't a crime."

"It could make you afraid of reality."

"That's nonsense!"

"Is it, Jane?" He took a step toward her and instantly she took a backward step, retreating from him before she could stop herself.

"You see," he jeered, "you're afraid of me be-

cause I'm real and not an actor with prescribed lines
of speech and action. I'm unpredictable because you
don't know what I'm going to say or do in the next
few moments."

"If you touch me I-I'll scream—"

"You wouldn't be heard, Jane. We're alone up
here in the Black Baron's Tower and the walls are of
Cornish granite and thick as a three-volume Gothic
novel."

"Oh—I'm not staying here to put up with this...."

"Of course you are!" His eyes mocked her. "No
one's ever spoken to you like this before and deep
down you're excited by it."

"That isn't true!"

"Isn't it, Jane?"

"It's insulting of you to imply that I'm enjoying this
situation. I-I'm doing it for the money."

"Right. And I expect value for the money I pay
out; I don't put up with any halfhearted effort from
the people I employ. Is that understood?"

"Yes."

"Then we'll have no more arguments about having
breakfast together like a pair of lovebirds, is that also
understood?"

"No."

"What an exasperating young creature you can be,
Jane. Would you argue like this with the director of a
play?"

"That would be entirely different."

"You mean if he wanted you to play a scene in bed
with your leading man then you'd play it without argument?"

"If the scene belonged in the play, yes." It wasn't
easy for Janie defying this man who towered over her
and could have picked her up with one hand and

given her a good shake, but somehow she managed it. "I don't see that it's necessary for anyone to see us in bed together a-and I won't agree to any such thing."

"But I insist on it, Jane." His voice had softened but his eyes had hardened and Janie had to force herself not to take to the bathroom, where there was a lock on the door.

"Why?" she demanded.

"Because when Roxanne shows up again I want it firmly understood by everyone that I'm no longer interested in her. They're bound to jump to that conclusion, just as they assumed—my sister included—that I'd killed her in a fit of rage. Love mad! That was the term they used about me at the time. Maybe then it fitted me, but it no longer applies and I'll have an end to the damned nonsense.... The legend that grew out of it all, as if Roxanne and I were a modern variation of Tristram and Isolde!"

"Maybe that's how the two of you struck people." Janie could see in him a kind of wild magnificence that the beauty of Roxanne would have complimented. They would have matched each other in looks and temperament, their life together as stormy as it was passionate.

Did he really believe that he could resist Roxanne if she returned to claim him?

"I know what you're thinking." He thrust a hand through his black hair, dislodging a strand so it fell across his brow. "That I wouldn't go to the extreme of providing myself with a talisman against the witch if I felt sure of my feelings. I don't feel sure of them, but I do know that I won't go through hell again for brief spells of heaven. I need her to believe that I've put someone else in her place...and Roxanne's favorite place was her bed, with me in it!"

The force of the words washed over Janie in a wave, making her feel breathless. She couldn't take her eyes from his face, in which power was equally blended with the passion Roxanne could stir into life even in her absence. He stared back at Janie and she saw the memories molten gold in his eyes.

"Will you refuse me, Jane?" He looked almost quizzical. "Can't you see that it's an integral part of the script that you be seen with me in the one place Roxanne regarded as her domain? It isn't enough that you be seen in my house. I want people to look at you, young, fair and just a little naive, and I want them to imagine you in my arms.... Mine, in all that it entails. I want that and I won't be refused!"

"Y-you won't touch me?" Janie was so tense in every limb that it actually hurt.

"Not even with a toe."

"Just to—to have breakfast?"

"Just that, Jane."

"All right, but if you dare break your word about...." She eased her dry lips with the tip of her tongue. "About not touching me, then I'll walk out on you. Do we have a bargain?"

"It would seem so, wouldn't it?"

"Promise!"

"My dear girl, have you some phobia about being touched? I may inadvertently brush your arm when I reach for the toast. Will that count against me?"

"I-I don't mean that kind of touching."

"What kind do you mean?"

"You know very well."

"You mean the intimate kind, eh? The prelude to the hard stuff?"

She flushed and looked away from his mocking eyes. "I know you think I'm being a prig, but I want your promise and that's that."

"What I'll promise, Jane, is that I'll behave as well as you can expect from a Pentrevah. We're rather a wicked lot, I'm afraid, and reformation doesn't come easy to a man who springs from a long line of Cornish barons."

Janie gave him an amazed look, and he bowed his black head. "It wouldn't do, would it, for you not to know that you're supposedly wed to the reigning baron."

"Truly?" Her eyes were fixed upon him, wide and wondering.

"Cross my heart, Jane." He swept a hand around the room. "You're living in the Black Baron Tower; did you think it was just a name?"

"I...suppose I did."

"The Pentrevahs go back a long way and some of them have been smugglers on the side, sailing across to Brittany at dark of night in order to pick up kegs of contraband cognac, bolts of fine lace, tea and tobacco. It was the fun of slipping past the excisemen they most enjoyed."

"Did they join in the wrecking, as well?" Janie now felt that nothing relating to this man would surprise her. A baron indeed!

"Those stories about wreckers are a load of rubbish. The Cornish folk were never so hard up for pickings that they deliberately put out false lights in order to lure ships onto the rocks. It happened too often without their assistance, for our coast is a rough and dangerous one, and if a ship wrecked itself then the spoils were considered their right as much as the seas. Some of the silver in this house has come by that way, and my den is paneled from some fine Spanish wreck wood."

"Is there Spanish blood in the Pentrevahs?" Janie studied his face in the ruby lamplight and thought again that he could pass for a Spanish hidalgo.

"You'll find it in families up and down this coast, not to mention a dash of the Arab and the Turk." A smile ran around his lips. "We're on the Atlantic so we've always been at the mercy of marauding ships. Long ago a Pentrevah girl was carried off. Her brother went hunting for her and finally he managed to ransom her back into the family. She came carrying a child; she had been used by the Turk into whose household she had been sold. The child was born and grew up as a Pentrevah, so doubtless I have a strain of the Turk in me, as well."

"The Turks had harems in those days, didn't they?" Janie was fascinated by what he told her; she had read of such happenings in novels but it was far more exciting to actually be told that girls had been carried off by pirates and placed in harems where they were forced to endure the attentions of the bey. A little shiver ran through Janie. Now she knew why Pagan Pentrevah looked as he did, and had a kind of arrogance in his attitude toward her.

"Are you wondering if I have inclinations along those lines?" he asked sardonically.

"Haven't you?"

He gave a slight shrug that could have meant yes or no. "It's something a lot of women would appreciate despite all their big talk. They'd thoroughly enjoy being kept in jealous seclusion by a man, but the problem is too many men believe all the big talk and shift their attention to their cars. The car can't talk back and when it gets temperamental it responds to a loving overhaul and purrs like a cat when it gets going. Women can be foolish creatures."

"You'd be cynical, anyway," Janie murmured, as if saying the words softly would somehow mute his possible anger. "Your own marriage was such a disaster."

"I don't accept the blame for that, dammit!"

He scowled down at Janie but she plunged on regardless. "Perhaps Roxanne felt driven to do what she did."

"She should have consulted me if she was in fear. I had the right to decide on the outcome, not to have her going to some quack who might have killed her, as well!"

Silence fell and Janie watched as Pagan's hand clenched around a post of the bed, gripping it until his knuckles had a bone-white definition under the tanned skin.

"It's possible there's some truth in that story about her mother," he said at last. "Roxanne had irrational impulses, and she liked playing tricks on people."

"So now you're playing one on her?"

"You could say that." He fingered the carving of the bedpost. "I won't let her disrupt my life all over again."

"You might not be able to help yourself," Janie said quietly.

"That's why I'm enlisting your help, Jane."

"From what I've heard of Roxanne I don't think I offer much competition."

"Don't you?" He reached out a hand and Janie jumped like a cat at a shadow. He took scant notice of her nervousness and pushed his fingers through her hair. "I'm just checking to feel if it's dry. Silk soft, isn't it, but why do you have it cut like a boy's?"

Janie's scalp was tingling, along with every other part of her. "I suppose Roxanne has hair down to her waist?"

"Naturally. In bed at night it draped her like a cape of flame."

"Her hair is red?"

"As a vixen's."

"And her eyes are green?"

"Yes, Jane, but unlike yours, hers are as deep and wild as the treacherous Atlantic."

He gazed down broodingly at Janie, as if comparing her in his mind—his senses—with the woman he had known so intimately and yet had not known at all.

"Do you know what I think, Mr. Pentrevah?"

"I'm all agog for the revelation, Miss Larue."

"I think you remember every detail about Roxanne and that you're really dying to have her back. You're letting your pride stand in your way!"

"The pride of a pagan, eh?"

"Yes." She tried desperately not to tremble as she felt his fingers slide down to the nape of her neck and press almost threateningly against her skin.

"What's a Pentrevah without his pride, Jane? He'll take by fair means or dark deeds, but he'll not kneel."

"What if it had been decided that you'd pushed her into Prowler's Pool?" Janie asked curiously.

"I wouldn't have begged them to believe that I hadn't."

"That's crazy!"

"Poor child, you feel you've wandered through a hole in the hedge and found yourself at the Mad Hatter's tea party, eh?" He tilted Janie's head and gazed down into her eyes. "Are you saying I belong in a crazy woman's arms?"

"No!"

"Maybe I belong in yours, Jane."

"No...."

"That was a little less definite, my dear. Don't you fancy the real thing in place of the make-believe? Aren't you just a little bit curious about this mad impulse that drives out sane, logical, dignified feeling and puts in its place the hunger to possess and be possessed?''

"I-I don't want to talk about it ... with you!"

"Little liar. You wouldn't be human if you didn't wonder about the hungers of the senses. We've all got them, Jane, and they're every bit as acute as our longings for bacon and eggs, or peaches and cream. You mustn't starve them, you know, or they'll give you an acid outlook on life."

He gripped her chin and all she was aware of was his dark face and the look in his eyes that was partly mocking and partly inquisitive.

"Don't let that happen, Jane, it might spoil the sweetness I see in your face."

Her heart jumped. No one had ever said anything like it before and it made her afraid of him again.

"Don't you want the hungry possession of a man?" he quizzed her. "Or don't you yet know what you really want?"

"I know very well what I want and that's to be a successful actress."

"Surely that doesn't rule out the desire for love?"

"You can't give your devotion to two things at once, and being an actress can be very demanding."

"More demanding than a husband?"

"More or less about the same."

"Not all actresses are single, are they? Or do they go in for affairs, enjoying love as a dessert rather than a main course?"

"You wouldn't really understand." She stood there tensely between his hands, too keenly aware that her sole covering was her pajamas and he could feel her skin beneath the light covering. Her skin warmed at the very thought, as if she stood too close to a fire.

"Do you take me for such a boor, Jane?"

"No, but you probably regard acting as a rather frivolous occupation."

"That wouldn't be very sensible of me, Jane, when you're here because of the acting."

"I-I don't think your sister's very impressed by your choice, or even convinced that we are man and wife."

"So now you know why I want to make things look a bit more definite."

"By being seen in my bed?"

"Exactly."

"That will only suggest that we're sleeping together."

"Right."

"So you don't really care if people aren't convinced that you've actually married me?"

"Do you mind, Jane?"

"Not particularly, except that it will hang a label on me when my job's done."

"Are labels all that important?"

"You didn't like the one they hung on you, did you?"

"Ah!"

"It wasn't nice, was it, being called a murderer?"

"No, Jane, but I knew the real truth, as you'll know it, that it's all been a game with cash in your hand at the end of it. The most valuable lesson you'll ever learn, my dear, is that it isn't necessary in this life to be liked."

"That's a very cynical point of view."

"I didn't say, Jane, that it isn't necessary to be loved. That is a very different kettle of pilchards."

Janie studied him, seeing mingled in his face the foreign strains from way back, and the shadings of arrogance that were inevitable in a man who had been

born in a Cornish *plas* that for generations had been
the Pentrevah stronghold, where each succeeding son
carried on the title of baron.

"I'm glad I'm not really your wife!" The words
broke from her in a heartfelt way.

"Thanks!" His smile curled the edge of his lip,
then was gone.

"You know what I mean."

"To each his own, eh?"

"Yes." Her toes clenched in the carpet and she felt
gauche in her pajamas, lacking in the glamour that
had been Roxanne's, reserved where the other girl
had been responsive.

"Don't compare yourself unfavorably with Roxanne, if that's what you're doing."

The words had a touch of the whip in them and
Janie flinched as if she actually felt lashed.

"Other people will compare me to her, and wonder
what you see in someone so different. Tristana told
me that she was the most beautiful creature from
Land's End to John O'Groats."

"Yes, she had everything it took to excite a man,
and send him halfway to hell and back. Having got
back I'll be damned if I'll chance another trip!"

All arrogance was let loose in him suddenly and he
swept Janie up in his arms and strode with her to the
head of the bed. Fear swept through her and she
struck at him and landed a blow against his jaw, which
was so hardboned that the blow probably hurt her
hand more than it hurt him.

"Put me down!"

"That's what I'm doing."

He slid her inside the covers, then leaned down
over her, his eyes mocking her fright and confusion.
"You have a certain naive charm, my dear, but I

won't ruin my chance of enjoying a leisurely breakfast with you. I'll leave you to have a restful night, but I'll be back in the morning.''

His eyes smiled wickedly as he took hold of her left hand, raised it to his lips and kissed it. "Sweet dreams, Jane.''

Speechlessly she watched him go to the door that led into his own room. He stood tall and dark in the aperture, his eyes intent upon her, as if he were remembering in her place a girl whose hair was a cape of flame around her white shoulders.

"Until the morning." The door closed behind him, and Janie's breathing gradually steadied. In a while she allowed her head to relax upon the pillows, but it was quite some time before she gathered the nerve to turn out the bedside lamp that left her in darkness, a drift of cheroot smoke coming in from the room next door.

She lay there going over all they had said to each other and from it all she distilled one pertinent fact... he still loved his wild Roxanne.

CHAPTER EIGHT

JANIE AWOKE to sunlight streaming through soft net. The big bed was so comfortable that she always felt rested, and yet as soon as her eyes opened she was alert to the fact that the door between these rooms would open any moment and a tall figure would stride in. His hair would be tousled on his brow, and his dark robe would be half-open against a brown chest where the black hair was distributed across the firm muscles and centered down toward the flat stomach.

For almost three weeks he had been joining her each morning for breakfast, but she still felt a thrill of alarm each time the door was thrust open and he took those long strides that brought him to her. At her bedside he'd throw off the robe and slide in beside her under the covers. Janie suspected that he slept in his own bed as naked as the day he was born, but as a concession to her modesty he wore pajama bottoms when he shared her bed so they'd be seen intimately together by the maid who brought their breakfast tray.

The morning sun made its way around the room as if seeking its golden reflection in the well-rubbed patina of the antique furniture, the cut glass lids of the twin powder bowls on the dressing table and the chased silver backs of the beautiful hairbrush set that Pagan said had belonged to his mother and which Janie could use. He further added that the hairbrush set hadn't been used by anyone else but his mother.

Janie had assumed that his mother was dead, like his father who had been killed in the war while in France as an agent with the partisans. A little too old at that time to join the services he had insisted upon doing something and because he spoke fluent French he had managed to be of considerable help to the secret army until his capture by the enemy. He had died without revealing the names of his associates and Pagan had said with pride that his father's name was upon the memorial to the fallen in the church at Penzance.

Then, with a more somber look in his eyes, he had revealed that his mother was a member of a Carmelite order across the Tamar. He had told Janie the story beneath the big portrait of his mother in the Amber Room downstairs, which was used as the family drawing room. In some ways, he said, Merlin Pentrevah had been almost as wild and willful as his own wife Roxanne. The death of her husband had quieted her but it hadn't quite subdued her Cornish spirit. It had taken the death of Pagan's young brother to do that. He had been in his second year at a Jesuit college where he had developed a yen for the priesthood and had talked with his principal and his mother about studying the doctrine in the hope of taking the strict vows of a Jesuit priest. Then one October evening at a Halloween party he had drunk some spiked punch and being unused to drink had become intoxicated and gone with a group of youths to a local pleasure house. It had been raided by the police and the boys had found themselves in trouble, with the result that all of them, including Jason Pentrevah, had been expelled from the college.

Jason, only seventeen at the time, had been stunned by his senseless behavior, which went against the very grain of the self-disciplined life that he wanted to achieve. Whether without thinking, or on purpose, he had walked across the railway lines just outside Penzance and had been struck down by the express train from London.

The shock of Jason's death had almost killed Merlin Pentrevah, who had doted on the son who had been less dominant than Pagan, more delicate in appearance, a dreamy youth who took things very much to heart. She had lain ill for many months and when she finally recovered her black hair had gone silver and she had quietly left the *plas* and entered a Carmelite nunnery in Devon.

Pagan told Janie that he saw his mother about twice a year. The order was a sternly enclosed one and he spoke with her through a grille. He barely recognized in the quiet, calm woman in nun's clothing the vivacious Merlin who had loved to ride, to give long weekend parties, and wear clothes from the best fashion houses.

It seemed to Janie, hearing of these things, that there had been very little real love in Pagan Pentrevah's life. His brave father had died when he was four so he barely remembered him, and his mother's best love had been given to his gentle brother. Probably she had thought that Pagan was big and strong enough to face life without any kind of crutch but had seen in her younger son the need for support. It occurred to Janie that Pagan probably loved his mother very deeply... the proof lay in the fact that he had married a girl so similar to her.

Janie lay thinking of these things until it suddenly dawned on her that Pagan was late coming into breakfast this morning.

The door that suddenly opened wasn't his. Plum

entered carrying a smaller tray than the usual one, with only one cup and saucer on it. Janie's senses responded to a tension in the air, but at the same time she slid into the place Pagan usually occupied, denting the pillow with her elbow as she sat up.

"Morning, ma'am." Polly Pelham had a smile that showed two large dimples in her cheeks, which were always ruddy with health and good humor. Her nickname Plum really suited her.

"It's a real summery one." She settled the legs of the tray across Janie's knees. "The pilchard trawlers are in down by the harbor and you should just hear them gulls, greedy wretches that they are!"

Janie poured her tea and added cream and sugar. There had to be a good reason why Pagan was absent from breakfast this morning. She wanted to ask Plum if she knew but it would seem a bit absurd for a wife not to know her husband's whereabouts.

"What have you brought me?" She lifted a lid and found some rounds of crisp French toast, scrambled eggs and ham. "Mmm, looks good—"

"Don't you mind, ma'am?" Plum stood staring at Janie, who looked lost on her own in the big double bed.

"Mind?" Janie held her teacup suspended. "What should I mind, Plum, on such a sunny morning as this?"

"That Mr. Pagan's had a telegram and gone off in his car to meet the train from London."

Janie's heart skipped a beat. "A telegram from whom?"

"Her who ran out on him and gave him all that trouble."

Oh, God, it couldn't be true!

Janie slowly lowered her cup to the saucer, for she

could feel her hand shaking and didn't want to spill tea all over the bed. She didn't want to believe what Plum had just told her.... She was here. Here in this very bed in order to stop Roxanne from entering Pagan's life again so what was he doing at the station? He couldn't be meeting her! It had to be a misunderstanding.

"The telegram can't have been from ... Roxanne."

"There's no doubt of it, ma'am." Plum's hands were crumpling her freshly starched apron. "Gardner's boy found it screwed up on the ground by the garage and he brought it indoors to show mom. Went very quiet did mom when she read it, then said she'd make you your favorite breakfast."

"That was kind of your mother, Plum." Janie heaved a sigh. So it had happened, Roxanne had called and Pagan had answered her call without a moment's hesitation. Janie felt a sharp stab of pain as she visualized him meeting that woman on the station platform, probably wrapped in furs and looking pleased with herself because he had left the side of his so-called wife in order to obey her summons. The edge to Janie's appetite was dulled but she made a show of not being too concerned about this event, dramatic as it might turn out to be.

"I expect she wants him to drive her to Ruthvyn Manor." Janie forked ham into her mouth and forced herself to eat it. "I was told that she was going to live there."

Tristana had been her informant a few evenings ago, strolling over to the piano where Janie was playing music-hall songs and casually asking if Janie knew "There was I, Waiting at the Church."

"She's after him again!" Plum exclaimed. "Begging your pardon, ma'am, but you're going to have to watch out for her."

"I know." Janie managed a smile and half a slice of golden-fried toast. "It's nice of everyone to be concerned about me."

"You're nice to us, ma'am." Plum was now trying to smooth the creases from her apron. "Mom says it's a pity you're no match for her."

"I know she's very beautiful—"

Plum tossed her head. "You can look fetching yourself, ma'am, especially in your new dresses. You look a real treat in the green velvet one that matches your eyes; sort of silvery green I call it."

"Thank you, Plum."

"You're welcome, ma'am, but she ain't, begging your pardon for speaking out. I was at school when all that trouble was stirred up when she vanished the way she did. Mom worked here then as cook and she said he had cause if he had done away with her. Awful rows they had, then she'd be all over him, getting her own way again and him giving it to her. Oh, ma'am, what are you going to do?"

"Fight her!"

"That's the spirit, ma'am." The fighting words seemed to please Plum as much as they shook Janie for speaking them. "Don't you let her take your man away from you. He's something special, Mr. Pagan is. Gentleman though he is he can wrestle with the toughest wrestlers in Cornwall and not be thrown on his back. That's why *she* wants him back! She's heard that he's wed again and she can't abide that!" Plum's cheeks glowed redder than they naturally were. "Don't you let her have him!"

"I don't intend to." Yet Janie knew that the ground she stood on was as shaky as Prowler's Pool, and that right this moment Roxanne could be casting her spell over Pagan all over again. Between him and Roxanne there had been a marriage, even if it had been dissolved by law. Between him and Janie there was only an agreement that could be snapped like a thread that had patched up the hole in his life that only Roxanne could fill, however tormentingly.

"Do the villagers talk much about her, Plum?"

"Yes, ma'am. They remember the way she used to gallop through the laneways on her horse Trojan. Killed him, she did! Set him at a fence that had spikes on it, and him an Arab and a gift to her from Mr. Pagan. Ripped his belly open on the spikes did poor Trojan, and Mr. Pagan had to let the vet put that lovely horse out of his torment. She stood there while the vet did it, dressed in one of them stylish riding habits. Green it was, green as holly leaves. Not a tear did she shed for Trojan when he lay on the cobbles dead, with his blood around him. She climbed into the saddle of Mr. Pagan's horse and galloped off across the moors on him."

Plum shook her head, her eyes never leaving Janie, tense and slender there in the enormous four-poster.

"She never cared a whistle on the wind about anyone. My cousin Sylvie was her maid and she reckoned her ladyship didn't bother about anything but keeping her looks. She'd spend hours in front of the mirror, trying out different ways of making up her face and styling her hair. She could curse like a tinker, and Sylvie had to take care when she brushed madam's hair. It was ever so long and thick and it got tangled up when she went swimming down in Spanish Bay."

Plum lifted the tray from Janie's knees, as if she saw them shaking. "She was always throwing things at Sylvie. Once it was a buckled shoe and it cut Sylvie's

cheek. Mr. Pagan was furious over that, but she had a
way of getting around people and often Sylvie came
home with something she'd thrown out of her wardrobe, or it would be a box of chocolates with only a
few of the soft centers missing. But that kind of gener-
osity meant nothing to her because everything she
had was bought by Mr. Pagan.

"Ma'am," the contents of the tray rattled as Plum
turned to the door, "I won't maid her if she gets back
in this house. I won't have my face cut by her shoes,
and I don't want her moldy old chocolates! I don't
mind what I do for you, but I want no part of her!"

"It won't come to that, Plum."

"Won't it, ma'am?" Plum stood in the doorway
looking at Janie, then she said with a rush. "It's a pity
you're not having a baby, ma'am. He'd not give you
up for the queen of Sheba if you had his child inside
you!"

The door closed and Janie lay there burning, yet
Plum was right. No other woman on earth would
beckon Pagan away from a wife who was having his
child . . . possibly his son, the next Pentrevah.

But I'm not his wife!

The words rang out loud and clear in Janie's mind,
and elsewhere in her anatomy—mainly her heart. *Oh,
no!*

She sat up straight, clenching her arms around the
knees she had drawn up defensively against her body.
She hugged herself against the invading forces of feelings she had held at bay until this moment. Now they
were all over her, hacking away at her defenses until
she crumpled back against the pillows in surrender to
what had happened to her.

She had gone and fallen in love with Pagan Pentrevah, and because she had never been in love before it

was utterly overwhelming. Especially right now, when he was meeting Roxanne again and the sun was shining on her hair and making a flame of it around her wild and wonderful face.

Janie buried her own face in the pillows, tormented by the images that slid through her mind. Roxanne would reach up and put her arms around his neck. He would breathe her perfume and capitulate to her demand that he kiss her, his mouth meeting hungrily the lips that smiled triumphantly.

Janie shivered and actually felt ill with jealousy and the despair of having let herself fall for a man so far removed from the career she meant to follow. A man she could never have in actuality.

Everything between them was a pretense. All of it unreal except the aching that went on inside her when she went downstairs an hour later, accompanied by Cedric, the Great Dane who had attached himself to her. His twin brother Carne was far more aloof and was disdainful of everyone except his master. This morning Carne lay stretched out upon the floor of the hall looking very moody because Pagan had gone off and left him at home—having something rather more important to do than taking a romp as far as the beach, which was roughly half a mile from the house, below the shelving cliffs.

Janie stood a moment in thought, hands in the pockets of her jeans with which she wore a simple shirt with a scarlet scarf tied at her throat. A touch of rebellion against what she felt for a man who swore he didn't want his ex-wife yet who couldn't resist the first opportunity to be with her again.

Janie felt torn in two. One half of her wanted to drive away fast on the road back to London, so she'd never have to look at him again. But the other half of her couldn't bear the thought of not seeing him again. Cedric thrust his great head at her and gazed at her with yearning eyes. He wanted to·go to the beach so he could get nice and wet from dashing into the sea after the driftwood she threw in for him to fetch.

"Come on then!" She made her way from the house followed by the dog, who gave a noisy bark to signal his pleasure. Five minutes later Carne had decided to join them, still with a sulky droop to his head as if his canine instincts warned him that something disturbing was in the air. The handsome pair of dogs were five years old so they had not been part of the Towers establishment when Roxanne had been its mistress.

"Oh, stop thinking about the woman!" Janie berated herself, and with her red scarf fluttering at her throat she made her way down the windy cliff steps to Spanish Bay.

It was a brilliant morning and the jade sea sparkled as if alight with silver flames, burning and dancing and destroyed in gushes of spume when they hit the rocks strewn at the edge of the sands.

Janie took deep breaths of the invigorating air and with the dogs in joyous pursuit she raced across the sands to where the water splashed like a fountain, wetting her skin and hair with its spindrift. Soon she had found two pieces of driftwood of equal size and had the two dogs dashing like mad to retrieve them. Janie liked to swim but wasn't allowed to unless Pagan was with her. The waters of Spanish Bay were beautiful to look at but they had a power to them that wasn't entirely trustworthy. Pagan knew these waters as he knew every inch of every acre he owned. He had been swimming in the bay since a very young boy, but he had firmly insisted that Janie was never to swim alone. She could have argued that Roxanne had done so, but he seemed fixed on the idea that Janie was less able to cope with the wilder elements of life.

She had been shown the infamous Prowler's Pool, so brightly green and mossy it seemed unreal that beneath those clumps of moss was a bog that could suck down a moor pony in a matter of minutes. He had pointed out the silvery bog plant, spiked with yellow flowers, which grew close by, and shown her also some little skull-cap flowers. Whenever she saw these growing she was to take warning that a bog was nearby. It was true that some bogs were fairly shallow and would reach only to the knees, but others were bottomless and anyone sucked into one was beyond aid very, very quickly.

Like love, she thought moodily, bending to pick up a sand-crusted shell, which her fingers brushed absently. You were sucked into that before you realized that you'd taken such a dangerous step and felt its demanding pull upon your body, its painful grip upon your heart.

She sank down on the sands and the two dogs joined her, panting from their efforts, their sleek coats steaming a little in the sun, their eyes fixed brightly upon her.

"It doesn't take much to make you pair happy, does it?" She stroked their great heads, receiving a lick from Cedric and a quizzical look from Carne.

"You'd better not love that man too much," she warned Carne, knowing full well that she was really speaking to herself. "He's besotted with someone he knew and loved long before you came on the scene. So you'd better cheer up, old thing, and not let him see that you'd like to howl."

Cedric yawned and settled down with his head on

his paws, but Carne looked into her face as if he understood every word she'd said to him. With a sigh she lay back on the sands and narrowed her eyes against the sun-shot sky. Such a sweeping length of bay, the water brilliantly blue with overtones of shimmering green. The sea broke upon the rocks, some of them so large that deep pools of water formed within their compass and were left there when the tide had thundered in and then withdrawn. The beach at low water always looked desolate. A strangely shining place edged with gold crimson and coppered silver, where fascinating seashells sometimes lay abandoned among clumps of sea pea.

The cliffs rose massively above the bay, and always there was the catlike mewing of the gulls and the restless energy of the sea. Spanish Bay was wild and beautiful so it wasn't any wonder to Janie that its owner should react to a woman with the same attributes.

Janie listened to the foaming welters of water coming and going against the rocks. She lay there motionless, her thoughts lost in the motion of the sea. Long ago ships under sail had foundered on these rocks and she could imagine the torn timbers and broken sails, the marble-white bodies of the drowned floating among the cruel rocks.

The waves unfurled themselves with a hiss and a roar, spraying the air with moisture. The downbeating sun drugged Janie's senses and she drifted off to sleep there beneath the cliffs, great granite slabs that had merged to form giant steps....

She woke abruptly and a giant seemed to loom above her, enclosing her in his shadow.

She lay there and felt boneless, her heart beating like a drum. The big dogs were prancing around him and Carne's bark was deep, as if to combine welcome with reproof.

"Hello, down there."

"Hello...." She sat up confusedly. "I fell asleep."

"Our sun and sea air can go to the head like a wild wine." He stretched out a hand and Janie felt him lift her to her feet without any effort. His fingers gripped hers as she tried to pull away. He gazed down at her, the expression in his eyes concealed by the shadow of his brows. Janie noticed that his suit was darkly severe and superbly cut, his shirt flawlessly white against his swarthy skin. He had obviously taken great care to look his best for his meeting with Roxanne.

"I hear you went to the station to meet the divinity," she said with an assumed flippancy.

"That's right." He narrowed his eyes and his fingers tightened on hers. "I had things to say to Roxanne, and I also wanted to make sure that she didn't arrive unexpectedly at the Towers."

"I see." Janie looked away from him and wished he'd let go of her hand. His touch had become too personal; it was no longer just his strength that she was aware of, it was his disturbing maleness. It made her feel vulnerable, and testy with herself for getting bitten by the love bug when she had tried so hard to avoid its bite. She could feel the fever in her veins and the weakness in her legs because Pagan stood close to her. She felt despairingly that she had a real case of galloping infatuation and just had to find a way to fight it off.

"I imagine your ex-wife was looking gorgeous." Her training as an actress had never been more needed and she managed to make the words sound almost careless.

"From head to toe," he agreed, and Janie could feel his eyes searching her face. "You don't appear to mind too much that I met her and drove her to the house she's leased for the summer."

"Why should I mind?" Janie met his eyes and secretly applauded her own performance. "It isn't as if I were really your wife and in a position to make a scene because you make yourself look handsome to meet your previous wife. Oh, dear, this all sounds very Noel Coward, don't you think? In a minute a concealed orchestra will start to play 'I'll See You Again.' "

"So you think it's one hell of a joke, do you?" His voice roughened and so had his grip upon her.

"It is rather funny." Janie gave a shrug. "One moment you're kidding everybody that you've married again, and the next moment you're streaking out of the house at Roxanne's beck and call. Anyway, I'm pretty well fed up with putting on an act and if you'll pay me off, then I'll be on my way. I don't suppose anyone will be surprised.... They've always known that the moment Roxanne showed up again, you'd be hooked on her line."

"I'll hook you on a line, you impertinent young sprat!" He shook her until she gasped for breath. "My sole object in meeting Roxanne this morning was to protect you against her. Oh, yes, so you can take that astounded look out of your eyes. I know her! She'd have come to the Towers and used all the ammunition in her arsenal to make you feel—"

"What I am?" Janie flung at him. "An inadequate imposter?"

"Yes," he agreed. "Those two things among others."

"A plain and pretentious intruder?"

"If you need to put it in those terms, Jane, so get it out of your system."

"I want to get out— Out of your life!"

Janie was almost crying, hating him for agreeing with her, loving him even as she wanted to be out of reach of all these new emotions that hurt so much. It had been presumptuous of her to suppose herself an actress before he had happened to her with all his big darkness, all his own love-hate for Roxanne. She had been acting out fictions on a stage but now she was aching with the real thing and she wanted the curtain rung down before the emotion and the tension got out of control.

"Let me go!" The panic pitched her voice almost to a scream and she began to struggle and kick. He held her by the arms bruisingly and something brazen burned in his eyes a moment before her repetitive cry was silenced by his lips, crushed to a whimper as he brought his mouth down hard on hers. It wasn't so much a kiss as a means of aggression and he was too strong to be denied anything but her submission to him. His hands found the slimness of her hips and he pressed her into him with a force that hurt, and he kissed her.... Kissed her until she felt faint from lack of breath.

The fight was drained out of her and she lay there silently, her face against his shoulder, knowing only that there had been no tenderness in him, only the desire to dominate.

She felt possessed, taken over by a force beyond her control. A sob shook her as she felt his arm wrap itself around her waist.

"I have to ask you to stay, Jane," he said, his

breath against her hair. "We struck a bargain and I'm not giving you a penny of what I promised you until you've fully earned it. Understood?"

"But I'm not up to the job."

"It was you who called yourself inadequate, not I." He held her away from him and raked his eyes over her distressed face. "You who called yourself an intruder."

"It's what I am," she said shakily. "Pagan, don't you see, you must love Roxanne terribly if you feel you need me around to...to protect you against your own feelings. Oh, it's laughable!"

But neither of them were laughing. Pagan's jaw was hard-set, almost arrogantly so, that strand of black hair astray on his brow. Even yet, even knowing how he strove against the temptation of Roxanne, Janie would have liked to brush that strand of hair back into place, and she would have liked even more the touch of his mouth on hers again, only this time with a need of her as tearing as his need of the woman who was forcing her way back into his life.

"I know I ask a hell of a lot of you, Jane."

"I-I suppose I have to meet her?"

He inclined his head. "Inevitably. She's out to satisfy her curiosity about you. Can you take it, Jane?"

"Have I any option?" Her eyes moved of themselves over his brooding dark face. Invulnerable, a stranger would have thought, but Janie saw the tense little muscle beating beside his mouth. His mouth that she could never look at now without knowing how demanding and merciless his kiss could be.

"Can I rely upon you?"

"I...suppose so."

"Be a little more definite than that, my dear." A sardonic smile moved in and out of his eyes. "In order to stop her from coming to the house uninvited, I've invited her to dinner on Friday evening."

"Oh, God!"

"Don't faint," he said mockingly. "You've walked out on a stage in front of an audience, so I'm sure you can cope with Roxanne. I need you to do this for me, Jane. I need you to act brilliantly. You'll hold my hand and gaze into my eyes just as a bride should, as if I'm the center of your entire being."

The breath caught in Janie's throat. "Who do you take me for?" she flared. "Sarah Bernhardt?"

"It's really going to take acting of that high standard?" He gave a brief laugh but there was no amusement in his eyes. "I'm stabbed to the heart, Jane. I rather flattered myself that you didn't quite dislike me."

"It doesn't do to jump to conclusions." Janie felt a desperate need to hide her true feelings from him. If he had any inkling of them, then she'd be lost, sunk, at the mercy of whatever he asked of her. She wouldn't let herself be used by him and then tossed aside when Roxanne finally got him back.

"So you don't like me, Jane?"

"You said yourself that it isn't necessary to be liked."

"So my words are flung back in my face, eh?"

"There you are." She gazed out to sea, resolved to hold onto her pride even if her foolish heart had gone and given itself to him without the permission of her common sense. "We haven't a lot in common, have we? People need to have that if they are going to be...friends."

"Friends, Jane?" He quirked an eyebrow. "Is that possible between a man and a woman?"

"It has to be," she said quietly. "Without it life

wouldn't be supportable. How can you live closely with someone without friendship?"

"Haven't you heard of passion?" he mocked.

"I've heard of it, but I'd sooner be warm by a fire than burned up by it."

He stood silent, his gaze lost in the cool distances of the sea and the sky. She allowed herself a quick look at him, seeing a profile that was stern and bold and sun brazened, fit to be stamped on an old Celtic coin. A rush of unwanted feeling swept over her, a tingling in her bones and at the very roots of her hair. Emotion of a kind that could break down her resolves just as the sea broke in spinning drifts of moisture and light on the dark rocks.

"Is that a bit of your own wisdom, Jane, or did you read it in a book?" he asked abruptly.

"It's what I feel," she replied. "A flame is cruel if you get too close to it, but it can keep out the cold if you don't try to be part of it."

"Is that what happened to me, Jane? I got burned instead of comforted?"

"You know what happened to you better than I."

"So you'll see me burned again, Jane, without coming to my aid with a dash of cool water?"

"Smoldering fires aren't easy to put out." Janie summoned a smile. "You might need a fire brigade for that."

"I might, Jane, but I'm willing to take a chance on you, if you will take one on me."

"Meaning that I have to meet Roxanne and pretend I . . . love you?"

"Don't say it like that, as if the words burn your tongue."

"Lies usually have that effect on the tongue," and this time she was lying and the effect was painful.

"Will pretending be so hard?" Suddenly he had hold of her again and her slim body was pressed to his masculine hardness. All the strength seemed to leave her legs and it was just as well that he was holding her. A slight wind blew along the shore and the sound of the sea was loud, but not as loud as the beating of her heart.

"You're close to me now," he said, "is it so unbearable?"

She shook her head mutely. Being close to him was heaven and hell fire.

"You're shivering," he exclaimed. "By hell, I've never had that effect on a girl before. Or is it the thought of my ex-wife that gives you weak knees?"

It was his doing, his touch, his infuriating hold on her that she couldn't seem to break. A force beyond her control that had taken over her impulses and her actions. She was possessed by him, as if her personality had been split in two, one half of her wishing for escape, the other half held as easily as he might hold a kitten by the scruff of the neck.

"It's a long time since breakfast," she managed to say. "I expect I'm hungry and could do with some lunch."

"Yes, that's it." He spoke in the indulgent tone of a parent with a child whose mood rather eluded him at the moment. "I think you need to get away from the house for a couple of hours so we'll go and lunch at a seashore pub I know. Would you like that, Jane?"

"Oh, yes!"

"Come along then." He took her by the hand and called the dogs who were barking at a crab that was inching its way along the sands, and possibly feeling, Janie thought, as trapped as she by this towering man who was hastening her toward the cliff steps. He

bounded up them and when they reached the summit
Janie was breathless but had regained some of the
composure she had lost down on the beach with him,
where the looming cliffs had seemed to shut them
away from the world together.

"Should I go and change?" She eyed his smart suit.
"I had a romp with the dogs and I feel in a bit of a
mess."

"It's up to you." His eyes flicked over her. "You
look all right to me."

"I feel like a scarecrow." She combed her fingers
through her hair and into her mind stole an image of
Roxanne looking soigné from head to toe.

"Very well, run indoors and smarten yourself up,"
he said rather curtly. "Don't be all day about it, I
didn't have any breakfast."

"Too bad." She flung the words over her shoulder
as she ran from him toward the towers of his house,
etched in their moorland granite against the sky. He
had been in too much of a hurry to meet Roxanne to
bother about eating, yet despite all the obvious signs
that he wanted her back, he persisted in fighting her
off.

Janie hurried into her room and tugged off the things
she had worn on the beach. If Pagan was feeling the
same sort of inner tumults that she was feeling, then
she felt sorry for him. Love had to be reciprocated in
order to be enjoyed, without that it was just a pain you
wanted to be rid of as soon as possible.

Freshened and changed into a cream dress with a
jade green belt, Janie walked through the sunlight to
where Pagan waited beside a vintage Jaguar that was
obviously kept in superb condition by himself, for she
hadn't seen a chauffeur around the place. For all that
he was landed gentry Pagan Pentrevah was no idler,

no eater of the lotus while others toiled. He often worked long hours on the home farm and there were times when he took it into his head to go out with the trawlers who brought home the pilchards. He had vital energies that had to find their outlet, and as Janie drew near to him she felt again a stabbing awareness of how big and dark and demanding he was.

"In with you." His hand brushed her skin as he assisted her into the car, and his eyes met hers for a brief yet intent moment. "How quickly the young can renew themselves—like a tarnished gold chain that can be made shining new just by a dipping."

He strode around the Jaguar and entered by the other door. He slammed it shut and started the engine, filling Janie's eyes and thoughts as she sat there beside him. She knew what he was wishing, that hearts like bodies could be scrubbed clean of their clinging grains of desire and corrosive memory.

They took a road with a sheer drop at the side of it and Janie's fingers curled around the leather strap on the door beside her as Pagan allowed the needle on the speedometer to mount to eighty. The car seemed to leap hills and dips with the ease of the animal for which it was named. They sped through countryside of a wild beauty Janie would have liked to study. The top of the car was open and the warm air danced through her hair and ran its touch over her bare neck and arms, her dress being a sleeveless one.

Janie made one or two remarks but Pagan barely answered her. Being wrapped in his thoughts, she supposed, of his previous companion in the car.

What had he and Roxanne discussed after all this time? What had been her reaction when he had told her about his supposed remarriage? Had she been as skeptical as Janie felt sure everyone else was? It was

just that Pagan was Pentrevah of the Towers so no-
body dared to say outright that he was merely amusing himself with a young bit of stuff and passing her
off as his wife.

A tremor ran through Janie. There was probably
little doubt in Roxanne's mind that there was no real
obstacle in her way back to Pagan's heart and house.
She had relatives in the area and they would probably
have told her about the "little mouse" that Pagan was
cohabiting with. Roxanne would smile to herself, well
aware of her flamelike beauty that few other women
could outshine.

Hadn't Pagan said himself only a short while ago
that Roxanne was still gorgeous!

The car headed down a slope toward Clune Harbor.
There were quaint shops at either side of the sloping
road and a tang of fish in the air. A variety of seacraft
lined the cobbled seawalls of the harbor and Janie
could see that this old-world place hadn't changed
much in a hundred years. She liked what she saw and
was grateful to Pagan for suggesting they lunch here
and not at the house. She needed time in which to
adjust to the curiosity and speculation that Roxanne's
return to the neighborhood had already aroused.
People would be watching avidly to see which way the
wind blew and whether there was smoke and sulfur in
the air. None of it would have affected Janie had she
kept a guard on her heart, but at some time during her
stay at the Towers she had allowed Pagan Pentrevah
to unguard her and now she couldn't even look at him
without a thrill to her nerves that was as painful as it
was pleasurable.

He braked the Jaguar in the courtyard of an inn that
was all white and black like a medieval chessboard.
Janie let herself out of the car before he could do it
and maybe touch her again. She had to be careful and

the last thing she wanted was for him to guess that he had so disturbing an effect on her.

The courtyard was paved with old worn cobbles, and the windows of the inn were mullions that time and weather had scarred and hung with ivy. It looked like the kind of place that smugglers had used in the old days, and the interior didn't disappoint with its blend of smoky oak, pewter and ale from the barrel.

A stout sea-tanned landlord came around from the bar to greet Pagan who, after shaking hands with him, introduced Janie by name without, thankfully, adding that she was his wife.

"I want Jane to sample the best grilled pilchards in this part of Cornwall," he smiled as they were shown into a paneled booth with oak seats and a table to match.

"Aye, and maybe the young lady would like to taste our blackberry wine?"

"What do you say, Jane?"

"I won't say no."

Pagan quirked an eyebrow. "The wine for Jane, and I'll have a pint of your best ale. You still draw it from the wood, Hal?"

"Wouldn't serve my customers anything else, sir."

"Do you still serve your famous figgy duff?"

The landlord chuckled. "Your sister was in here last week eating it.... Never could resist my roly-poly fig pudding, could she?"

"True." Pagan's gaze dwelt on Janie. "You'll have to try a helping, my dear."

"Sounds nice." Janie braced herself against his eyes and his casual endearment. "And I must admit I'm ravenous."

"Our Cornish air is famous for sharpening the appetites, isn't that so, Hal?"

"The young lady isn't one of us, sir?"

"No." Pagan's eyes dwelt intently upon Janie so that she had to fight for the composure to sit there and look as if she wasn't disturbed to the very depths of her being. She could feel his eyes probing into her as if he sensed the unrest inside her that her cool outer self concealed. She bore his scrutiny though it took some doing and breathed a sigh of relief when he turned his attention to the menu.

It was a lunch she wasn't likely to forget in a hurry, shared with Pagan in the precincts of this old inn lost in time. The grilled pilchards were tasty beyond description, then they had pork roasted with apple and onion and served with baked potatoes, parsnips and peas. Janie felt she couldn't eat another crumb but Pagan insisted that she have a slice of figgy duff, over which was poured a generous helping of Cornish cream with the tang of the sea in it.

Janie sat back with a sigh of repletion and heard Pagan laugh softly, as if to himself.

"I'm glad I amuse you," she murmured.

"You're still such an unawakened child, aren't you, Jane?" He put a flame to his cigar and blew the smoke softly away from him so it teased her nostrils.

"Because I still enjoy the simple pleasures?" she asked. "I like this place and I shall remember lunching here on real Cornish fare."

"I'll remember," he murmured. "Already you look ahead to days when we'll be apart from each other, don't you?"

"Of course." How it hurt to realize it and to say it. "It wouldn't do for me to believe the fiction rather than the fact—not that I think that anyone is really convinced that you're married to me. You're Pentre-vah so they don't argue with you, but I believe everyone's got me taped as your mistress."

"Why, Jane, should people find it so hard to believe that we aren't really wedded?" The cigar smoke wreathed around his features and lost itself in the blackness of his hair. He seemed to Janie to be well at home in the environs of the Sea Gull Inn where long ago contraband goods had been stored in its cellars after being landed stealthily in the harbor.

There were people born out of their time and Pagan was one of them, and a suspicion entered her mind that she might be another. Janie only knew that the so-called liberated antics of actresses she had worked with had left her with the feeling that it was all rather a sham, and a shame. She wasn't like them. It wasn't mere prudery but she couldn't have entered into a light relationship with a man just for the fun of it, or because it was considered the fashion. She inwardly winced at the thought that people took her for Pagan's light of love but nevertheless she had his welfare at heart. She cared that he was in torment over his marriage that had foundered on such sharp and wounding rocks. It was because he had been deeply hurt by the wreck that he caught at any chance line that might drag him clear of a second submersion into the choking depths of misery.

She, Janie, was that lifeline. Not a very substantial one, and one that might break in his hand, but he had hold of her and she couldn't fight him. When she looked at him, into his eyes that were smoky gold at the moment, she didn't want to fight, she just wanted to surrender.

"Why," he repeated, "should it seem so impossible that you and I should be man and wife?"

"Because of the comparisons," Janie said quietly. "People always make them. It's the same in the theater. If one actress has played a certain part and left her personality upon it, then the actress who follows in her steps must accept that the audience will compare her performance with the original, her looks, voice and mannerisms, also. How, Pagan, do I compare to Roxanne, or compete with her?"

"By being yourself, my dear."

A vagrant smile touched her lips. "That's exactly the sort of reply I'd expect from a man."

"The one thing I can't help, Jane, is being a man. Does it scare you so much, even though we've shared breakfast together a number of times?"

"Oh, I know you've managed to convince your household that we sleep together, but they aren't convinced that it's legal."

"Would you like it to be made legal, Jane?"

"It isn't a matter to be joked about!"

"Who's joking?"

"You have to be!"

"Do I? Are you now going to fling at me that hoary old chestnut about not marrying me if I were the last man on earth?"

"Marriage is a serious matter and you know it. Anyway, I have my career and you're still in love with Roxanne."

"I've been finished with Roxanne for a long while." He flicked ash from his cigar but Janie wasn't convinced that the gesture included his ex-wife. "If she's the reason you're refusing me, then forget her."

"Really, Pagan, you tell me to forget her but you're the one who must do that before you ask someone else to marry you. I begin to think there's nothing you wouldn't do in order to revenge yourself on her. That's all it is, isn't it?"

"Vengeance shall be mine," he drawled. "You're convinced that's what I'm after?"

"Totally."

"Even though I'm prepared right now to go and order a marriage license?"

Janie gazed at him with reproving eyes. "Stop it, Pagan!"

"Am I breaking down your resistance, Jane? Just think of it, you'd be mistres of a Cornish *plas* and your name will be entered into Debrett—"

"Shut up!" Janie could stand no more and, jumping to her feet, she ran out of the dining room and sped across the courtyard in the direction of the shops. She wasn't aware of a car that was at that moment turning into the courtyard of the inn and even though the driver hastily applied his brakes, one of the bumpers struck her and hurled her to the ground. Fear and pain blended and as a tide of darkness swept over her it was broken for a dazzling instant by the sound of her name, shouted loud and anguished.

"Jane!"

CHAPTER NINE

JANIE WAS ALLOWED OUT OF HOSPITAL a few days later. She had sustained some painful bruising and a bump on the head but when it was decided that she wasn't concussed Pagan brought her some fresh clothing and drove her home to the Towers.

"Whatever made me run into that car?" she remarked as he swung the wheel of the Jaguar and they drove beneath the trees that lined the driveway to the Towers.

Pagan didn't answer her until he brought the car to a halt in front of the house. The sun played over its high granite walls and lighted the mullioned windowpanes. Janie felt a sense of pleasure and homecoming. Then she felt Pagan lean toward her and she looked at him.

"It was something I said, wasn't it?" he murmured.

"Was it that bad?" She smiled slightly. "I've been racking my brains to remember. What was it you said?"

He stared at her, and Janie gazed back into the eyes that were tawny gold and startling in his dark face. She had felt a bit hazy minded those first couple of days in hospital in a private room where a young nurse had waited upon her hand and foot. It had startled her to be referred to as Mrs. Pentrevah but directly Pagan came to see her, striding so tall and dark to her bedside, Janie had known he was her husband.

"You don't remember, Jane?" A thoughtful frown joined his black eyebrows together above the forceful nose, and the bold chiseling of the mouth she longed to feel again on hers.

"I-I've a vague idea it had something to do with someone you'd invited to dinner." Her hand stirred, found his sleeve and traveled up his arm to his shoulder. "You'd better tell me again, Pagan, and this time I'll try not to act the fool."

"It was Roxanne." He watched her intently, his eyes upon her like a hawk's.

"Roxanne!" Her fingers gripped his shoulder. "Of course. Silly of me to forget, but now it comes back to me. I was upset because she's your former wife and I'm scared of meeting her. Did I accuse you of still being in love with her?"

"Yes, Jane."

"Oh, dear." Janie traced a finger down his grooved cheek. "So that was why we had words. I'm sorry for behaving like a fool. You must have been angry with me."

"I was concerned for you. Jane, are you sure you feel all right? The doctor assured me—"

"I'm perfectly all right." Impulsively she leaned forward and kissed his face. "My bruises are fading and my head has stopped aching. I wanted to come home—with you."

"Did you?" Still he watched her, seemed about to say something else, then changed his mind. He let himself out of the Jaguar, then came around to assist Janie, whose legs still felt a little tremulous. She took a deep breath of moorland air and her gaze roved the Towers, so exactly the kind of house a man like Pagan should live in. When she had realized with a thump that he was her husband, it had no longer seemed to matter that she had always wanted to make her mark

as an actress. When he had leaned over her hospital
bed and kissed her forehead, the most tremendous
surge of joy had lifted her heart on its crest.

She felt it again as she walked with him into the
enormous hall of the *plas* with its great beams overhead, its paneled monk stalls, its gleam of solid oak
and tall windows emblazoned with the figures of
saints. She breathed beeswax and sun-warmed stone,
and then abruptly she felt a chill that seemed to reach
to the very bottom of her spine, a finger of ice that
froze her to the spot.

Someone was seated on the oak coffer that stood
beneath the portrait of the Pentrevah who had built
the *plas* all those years ago. The woman was too vivid
to be a ghost, and Janie had never known of a ghost
that smoked a cigarette in a holder.

The scarlet lips drew smoke into them, and then
slowly released it so it twined upward into a flame of
hair that was fingered by sunlight through the stained-
glass windows. Long legs in sheer hose were crossed
seductively, and there was a look of ease and assur-
ance about the figure that made Janie seethe with re-
sentment. "Get out!" she wanted to say. "You don't
belong here anymore!"

"Roxanne!" Pagan's voice seemed to hit the beams
above their heads.

"I came to welcome home the bride." Roxanne
rose to her feet with a lazy sort of grace. "I heard
she'd had an accident—poor dear."

"You've got a damn nerve!"

Janie shot a glance at Pagan and saw that he had
gone ashy around the nostrils, his eyes glittering with
anger. Impulsively she tucked her arm through his
and gave Roxanne a steady look.

"I'm perfectly all right now," she said, and was

pleased that her voice wasn't as shaky as her knees. "It was only a minor accident, just a few bruises and a bump on the head. I should have been looking where I was going."

"Which I'm sure you usually do." Roxanne flicked her dense green eyes up and down Janie's slim figure in the simple beige suit that emphasized her youth. "I'm sure when you set your sights on something—or someone—you don't usually fall over, unless it's with eagerness to reach your goal. I was informed that you act. Do you?"

"I did," Janie replied, and it was a relief that Roxanne didn't offer to shake hands. "Naturally I've given it up now I'm married."

"Naturally." Roxanne's eyes flicked green and sharp to Pagan. "As I remember—all too well—Pagan was always the sort to expect his wife to be solely interested in him. Have you found that he suits his name?"

"Only too well," Janie murmured, feeling the tenseness in the muscles of Pagan's forearm, as if she had welded herself to warm steel.

"Such a great big man for such a little girl to manage." Roxanne gave a silky laugh and there was insolence rather than amusement in her eyes. "I can imagine you in *Midsummer Night's Dream*, but not in anything really passionate."

"Such as *Cat on a Hot Tin Roof*?" Janie queried, looking innocent.

The green eyes narrowed to gleaming slits in the near-perfect face. The tip of her tongue ran itself around the glossy lips as Roxanne stood there in a lynx jacket of pale spotted fur, the jacket draped back from a dress high at the neck and yet suggesting every hidden curve of her figure. She had smooth unlined skin stretched over defined cheekbones, the sharp arching of her eyebrows reached toward the flaming hair that would always have had a will of its own. The tremblous shadow of her lashes revealed and then concealed the gem-colored eyes. Her eyes were those of a sorceress and would always have cast spells over men.

Janie looked at her rival and felt as inexperienced as a girl not long out of school. Even the feel of Pagan by her side, even the weight of his ring on her marriage finger couldn't dispel the threat that exuded from Roxanne.

She had great beauty and attraction, there was no use denying it. For Pagan to see her in his house again could only set fire to his smoldering memories of her when she had lived here as his wife.

Jealousy stabbed through Janie and she barely suppressed a gasp of pain. She couldn't compete with Pagan's memories of his marriage to Roxanne, and though her arm was linked with his, she felt afraid for her tenuous grip on his heart. He had married her not from love but to form a barrier against this woman. But, oh, what a flimsy barrier he had chosen! Roxanne knew it and let her knowledge show in her eyes.

"Be a little more welcoming, Pagan." Roxanne rested a hand on her hip, a huge stoned ring sparkling against the pale fabric of her dress. "I was invited to dine remember, and then told not to come because your wife had had her little accident. Why did you run in front of a car I wonder?"

The green eyes had shifted to Janie and the cigarette in its holder was raised to the full red lips. "On my honeymoon with Pagan I wasn't doing any running, least of all under the wheels of a car."

"It wasn't deliberate," Janie felt her hatred of this

woman growing and spreading inside her. Her exotic beauty had a venom in it, like some lush flower whose sap could cause harm to whoever handled her. Janie pressed herself closer to Pagan, as if to let him know that she understood his feelings. He made no kind of response with his own body and her heart felt chilled. It was as if with Roxanne in the room he was unaware of anyone else; she had shared so much more with him than Janie ever had. He had loved her in this house and out there on the moors, and it was in human nature to forget pain more quickly than pleasure.

"Are we ever sure whether our actions are deliberate or not?" Roxanne drawled, flicking ash to the floor. "We do things impulsively, and then regret them for years. Wouldn't you agree, Pagan?"

"It's in some people to be impulsive, in others to be calculating," he replied.

"When you say that to me, darling, I have such a feeling of déjà vu. Did you say it to me once before?"

"I believe I did."

"Of course, you did. Like me, you probable remember the minutest detail of the year we lived together. Only a year and yet it has left such an impression upon us."

"Speak for yourself, Roxanne," he rejoined. "We both married other people, didn't we?"

"True." She gave a shrug as if to dismiss those other people. "James died. He had a controlling interest in a dozen corporations so I won't starve, except for affection. Do you think I shall be on short rations where affection's concerned?"

"I never knew it was affection you hungered for, Roxanne."

"You never called me Roxie like other people, did

you, Pagan. James did." She wrinkled her perfect nose. "He was a genial man but he never quite had your style. As I said the other day, darling, you're looking very tanned and fit."

"And you continue to look beautiful."

He said it in an ordinary tone of voice but it made Janie feel bleak, suddenly almost a stranger who had less right to be in this house than Roxanne who had graced it with her vivacious presence. Janie could feel herself shrinking away from Pagan. Suddenly she felt tired, and felt that the house was huge and stony and hostile. That coming-home feeling had melted right away and her head had begun to ache slightly. She could almost wish herself back in hospital with its comfort and kindness. She hadn't dreamed of walking into a confrontation with Roxanne at this time, when she was still feeling shaky.

Why couldn't the woman behave with a little more sensitivity? Pagan had remarried, yet still she came here, acting as if she still had a hold upon him that reduced Janie's to insignificance.

"You look rather wilted, dear." Roxanne was looking at Janie as if willing her to wilt right away so she could stretch out her scarlet-tipped hand and fasten it upon Pagan.

"I probably need a cup of tea to revive me." Janie forced some life back into her voice, and it took a hellish amount of courage to add, "I'll go and have it in my room, you two probably want to talk and can have yours down here."

Janie drew her arm out of the crook of Pagan's and he didn't attempt to restrain her. "Yes, go upstairs and rest, Jane," was all he said.

"We'll meet again," Roxanne drawled.

"Good afternoon," Janie said, and as she walked

toward the staircase she could feel green eyes boring
through her shoulder blades, forcing her to draw upon
every ounce of her stage experience in order to mount
the stairs like a young bride instead of the dispirited
outsider that she felt.

Upon reaching her room Janie entered with a sigh
and sank down into the big armchair near the bed
whose tall carved posts reached almost to the ceiling.
Her gaze dwelt thoughtfully upon the bed. She had a
distinct impression of sharing it with Pagan, yet there
was a curious emptiness inside her, as if whatever had
occurred between those pristine sheets had been lacking in warm and turbulent passion.

In a short while Plum brought tea and cakes and
placed the tray on the round table beside Janie's chair.
"You look whacked, ma'am." Plum removed Janie's
shoes and replaced them with slippers. She poured a
cup of tea and added two spoonfuls of sugar.

"Thank you, Plum." Janie sipped the tea grate-
fully.

"She had no right coming here!" Plum exclaimed.
"She don't belong here no more!"

"Try telling her that," Janie said with a weary little
smile. "She's so outlandishly beautiful that she obviously does just as she pleases and for the most part
gets away with it."

"But it isn't right, ma'am. This is your house not
hers!"

"I wonder." Janie's gaze roved around the big,
handsome, clean-smelling room into which stole the
sounds of the birds on the moors, swooping and
calling above the buttergold broom, the lonesome
rocks and wind-twisted rowans. Janie wanted to smell
only the fresh tang of the moors but there still clung
to her nostrils the scent of the ambergris that had

clung around the figure of Roxanne. Still Janie's mind was filled with the image of her, in the dress whose fluid grace hinted at silky-firm curves. An animal grace of movement that men would be drawn to follow to some secret place where they'd plumb the depths of a passion such as Pagan had shared with her.... *With her*, Janie thought bleakly, *but never with me.*

It seemed ages to Janie before Pagan came to her room. She knew he would and was seated at the dressing table in her robe, buffing her fingernails and trying to look nonchalant.

Through the mirror she saw the door open and saw him framed there a moment before he closed it deliberately behind him. She tensed all through her body as he came and stood behind her so his eyes met hers in the mirror.

"You behaved admirably, my dear," he murmured. "You deserve a reward for courage, but I hope you don't feel too shaken after that encounter with the enemy?"

"I feel all right." Janie managed to sound quite convincing. "I expect you found plenty to say to each other?"

"You should have stayed and listened."

"I know when I'm not wanted."

"Nonsense!" His hands closed on Janie's shoulders but right now she didn't want him to touch her and she shook him off.

"Have you got the sulks?" he demanded. "You went off and left me alone with her, let me remind you."

"I-I couldn't stand the way she was looking at me." Janie buffed her nails with a fury that matched the beating of her heart. "She wants you back and she isn't going to let me stand in her way. She made me feel as if I don't belong here, as if she still has the right to come and go as she pleases. She knows she's the sort of woman that gets under a man's skin."

"And you aren't?"

She felt he mocked her and she kept her head lowered less she should see a reflection of that mockery in his eyes. She quivered as she felt him brush a hand across her hair, still slightly damp from her shower. "Don't shrink away," he commanded. "How do you expect to arouse a man if you won't allow him to touch you?"

"I-I don't care for pretense—" She wrinkled her brow as a pain stabbed her temple. Something nagged at her mind but she couldn't seem to pin it down. It was a question and an answer at the same time, but neither would formulate and become clear to her.

"You look fetching in your robe so why should I pretend?" Pagan's fingers slid to her shoulder and gripped, though not tightly enough to hurt her. It compelled and reached down inside her, melting her into the submission she had felt ever since their meeting on the moors. How clearly she remembered him astride his horse, almost riding her down in the tall grass, yet the most important aspects of their relationship eluded her.... Their wedding day... and night.

It alarmed her that she had forgotten things since that stupid incident in the parking lot of the Sea Gull Inn. But if she dared to tell Pagan, then he'd insist on her seeing the doctor again and she didn't want to be ordered back into hospital... now, of all times, when Roxanne had come openly to the house, and would come again.

I love him, Janie thought bleakly. *I won't let her have him to hurt again!*

"Do you want to see what I have for you?" he asked. "Let's say it's a coming-home present."

"I don't expect presents," she said shyly.

"Which makes it nice to get one, eh?" His hand moved to his pocket, found what it sought and laid it upon the dressing table in front of Janie. She caught her breath, it was a cameo brooch of a delicate girlish head and something about it assured Janie that it was genuine ivory.

"Oh, I couldn't—"

"You'd better."

"It's lovely." She picked up the brooch and ran a fingertip over the carved face in a frame of ringlets. "What do I say?"

"This." He picked her up from the dressing stool as if she weighed no more than a plucked fruit, he held her and closed his lips hard upon hers. There was a sweet violence to his kiss that she neither had nor wanted any control over. It did things to her that left her a willing slave to his every wish, her arms encircling his neck, her lips tremulous and softly flushed from contact with his.

His eyes watched her, the gold irises flickering behind the half-lowered lashes, jet black like his hair. His features were brooding, and he breathed deeply so she felt the rise and fall of his chest muscles through the soft fabric of her robe. Then with sudden resolve he strode with her to the bed and laid her down. She gazed up at him, watching as his hand went to his tie and loosened it. Her toes curled into the coverlet and a quiver of longing ran up her slender legs, up into her body, slim and pliant where the robe had opened. The sensation was so exquisitely intimate that she caught her breath. He was unbuttoning his shirt when she did that, and suddenly he stopped undressing, swore savagely to himself and turned on his heel away from the bed.

"What the hell am I doing!" he exclaimed.

"Pagan?" She raised herself and gave him a bewildered look. "What's the matter?"

"Me," he said savagely. "I can't make love to you, that's what's the matter!"

He strode off into the other room, slamming the door behind him with a finality that made Janie flinch. The trembling desire died away and left her feeling shivery. She drew the eiderdown around her and tears welled into her eyes and fell down her face.

The matter was that he couldn't feel for her the wild passionate longing that Roxanne aroused in him and always would. Roxanne knew it and that was why she had flouted all the rules of good behavior and come to the Towers so his new wife could see how beautiful she was, and how enduring was her effect upon a man, especially a man who had possessed her as a wife.

Janie felt a sad sense of failure. Love for a man was a pain instead of a pleasure when his interest lay elsewhere. The only certainty right now was that she loved Pagan but wasn't loved in return. With a little choked sigh she slid from the bed and went to the dressing table where the cameo lay. She picked it up and loved it because Pagan had given it to her, but, oh, how she craved for him to give himself. As in the heather on the moors he had given his body and his heart to Roxanne.

The spell had been cast then and there, as if the pagan elements in the earth had joined his spirit to hers. It sounded theatrical and at one time Janie would have thought so but now she was more tuned in to the mystery of love and anything relating to it seemed possible. She could believe now that men and women could suffer the torments of the damned in the interest of someone loved.

Her eyes dwelt upon the door to Pagan's room and though she ached to step across that threshold, fear of a second rejection held her back. Now she had seen Roxanne she could understand why he found her impossible to forget, and why he was determined to try.

Outwardly she was everything that a man could desire, but Janie had seen for herself that Roxanne was one of those people who could be unscrupulous because she lived by her own rules. Her beauty was her weapon and she used it without conscience to get whatever she wanted—as years ago she had deliberately made it look as if Pagan had thrown her into the quicksand.

Janie felt herself go cold again, as she had down in the hall when she had caught sight of that exotic figure perched upon the coffer. So perfect to look at.... So imperfect beneath the skin that was as finely textured as that of a camellia.

I hate her, Janie thought fiercely. *I'd hate her even if Pagan didn't love her!*

With this in mind she went across to the closet and attached the cameo brooch to her favorite jacket. It looked nice...her reward for facing up to Roxanne, an ordeal that wasn't yet over!

AN ASSUMPTION that was proved correct again and again in the days that followed.

Roxanne came to the Towers whether she was invited or not, and she always had a plausible excuse, that a gallop had brought her in this direction, or she had picked up a painting or a piece of china at a sale and Tristana had an eye for a bargain. Upon another occasion she had longed for a swim in Spanish Bay and had brought a picnic basket with her, which she insisted should be shared by Pagan and Janie down on the sands.

The galling thing was that she exuded such charm that it seemed churlish to deny her. Tristana's distrust of her was soon a thing of the past, and though on the surface the friendship looked innocent enough Janie felt certain Roxanne was lining up Pagan's sister in support of her campaign to win him back. As the summer days slipped away Janie began to feel that her tenuous hold on Pagan was slipping out of her grip. He and Tristana had so much in common with Roxanne. The three of them had an affinity with the wild moors and the sea. They were picturesque people to look upon and their passions were rooted in this place.

Janie felt so different from them, and was conscious of her girlish shape in contrast to Roxanne's when they were in bathing suits. Her skin seemed paler, her bones slighter, her skill in the water, and on horseback less spectacular.

Pagan had presented her with a horse named Fred, who had long dancing legs and a likable nature. He was almost a palomino, and very much a contrast to the bold black horse that Pagan rode, and the fiery chestnut that suited Roxanne's temperament as well as her mane of red hair. In the saddle she was eye-catching and rather reckless, which was how she came to be thrown one afternoon and had to be carried back to the Towers on Pagan's horse.

Her ankle was badly wrenched and they had to call a doctor to attend to her. Janie knew what would happen and it did. Roxanne looked so sorry for herself that Pagan felt compelled to let her stay on as a guest until her ankle healed.

When told, Janie groaned inwardly but tried to look as if her world wasn't falling apart. Roxanne had got

her way, she had got back into the house that once
had been hers. Her maid arrived with a trunkload of
her clothing and a pigskin case filled with cosmetics.
Janie watched their arrival with the helpless feeling
that she might as well pack her things and leave.

Just as she was thinking this the telephone rang and
she walked across the hall to answer it. A man was on
the line, he said his name was Hunt Lincoln.

"Look," he was decidedly North American, "am I
talking to Pagan's new lady?"

"I—suppose you are." Janie smiled involuntarily.
"I'm Jane, the new Mrs. Pentrevah."

"Jane." He gave a tolerable imitation of Orson
Welles. "One of my favorite names, and possibly the
best heroine in romantic fiction. How are you liking
Cornwall? Highly romantic isn't it? I understand that
the mother of the Brontës was a Cornishwoman."

"I believe she was." This was decidedly an odd
telephone conversation but Janie quite liked the
sound of the man. "May I ask who you wish to speak
to, Mr. Lincoln?" she asked.

"All in good time," he said genially. "Right now
I'm enjoying speaking to you Jane. Has anyone ever
told you that you have a charming voice and that over
the phone it caresses the ear?"

"I was once in a play with an American and he
could flatter the hind legs off a donkey, as well."

"Jane, you wound me. You really do have a lovely
voice and I'm betting the rest of you matches up. Pagan always had an eye for a mettlesome filly. How is
the old boy?"

"I don't consider him old, Mr. Hunt, and he's very
well indeed. Shall I bring him to the phone?"

"Not just yet, Jane. I think you know that I'm the
guy's best friend?"

"He has mentioned you, yes."

"Things are okay with him? Word got to me that he'd got himself married again but I kind of felt hurt that he didn't directly contact me."

"It was a whirlwind affair," Janie explained, trying not to let it show in her voice that she still felt hazy about the ceremony herself and would have appreciated a résumé of it, had she dared to let Pagan know that such a momentous occasion in her life had slipped from her memory. More than once she had striven to remember her wedding day but the actual details still eluded her.

"I'm pleased for him," Hunt Lincoln said sincerely. "It's what I hoped he'd do instead of boxing himself up with a lot of regrets because his first marriage didn't work out. You know about Roxanne I take it?"

"Yes." Janie felt her stomach sink at the very name. "Roxanne is in the house right now. She took a tumble from her horse, hurt her ankle and is installed here while it mends."

"Good grief!" Silence hung on the line for a moment. "Look, I'm inviting myself to join the house party, okay with you, Jane?"

"Oh, yes," she said fervently. She had yet to meet Hunt Lincoln, yet she felt he was on her side, that he was possibly one of the few men who had managed to steer clear of an entanglement with Roxanne. "Please come!"

"I'm on my way, Jane. I shall probably see you sometime tomorrow."

"Shall I tell Pagan you're coming?"

"N-no, let my arrival come as a surprise all around. Goodbye for now, and keep your guard up."

"I daren't lower it, Mr. Lincoln."

"The name is Hunt. I'll see you!"

He hung up and Janie was left with the warm feeling that she had an ally in this friend of Pagan's. There had been in his voice a note of genuine pleasure that Pagan had married her, but he had obviously guessed that she was no real match for Roxanne, whom he had known in the old days. Knowing her, he had guessed that she was intent on causing mischief.

"Who was that on the phone?"

Janie gave a start and swung around to face Tristana.

"Ye gods, from the look on your face, Jane, it must have been a secret lover."

"It certainly was not," Janie protested.

"Then why look so guilty?" Tristana stood there with her hands in the pockets of her riding breeches. "When you come to think of it, we don't know an awful lot about you, do we, Jane? Before you came here you could have had all sorts of odd friends in the theatrical profession."

"I had friends but they weren't odd," Janie said with spirit. "They certainly weren't mischief-makers—like Roxanne."

"Even so, you are something of an unknown quantity, Jane, and still waters run deep. Who were you speaking to?"

"I don't have to tell you, I'm not one of the maids."

"Be secretive about it and take the consequences."

"What is that remark meant to imply, Tris?"

"That I might go and tell Pagan that I caught you chatting on the phone in a very confidential way. He'll want to know who the man is—"

"Why are you out to try and make mischief between Pagan and myself? Has Roxanne put you up to it?"

Tristana drew her left hand from her pocket and glanced at the face of her wristwatch. "I'm dying for some tea—"

"We both know she's out to make trouble," Janie said tensely.

"Do we?" Tristana touched the scar on her cheek, a nervous gesture.

"She wants Pagan back and she doesn't care what tricks she uses in order to get him, and everything that goes with him. If you cared about your brother, Tristana, you wouldn't side in with her but would be on my side. I care about his happiness. All she has ever done is make him unhappy. Is your memory so short? Have you forgotten the things she did to him?"

"I think she had her reasons."

"Even so," Janie said quietly, "she should have been open with him and not gone behind his back the way she did. His child was involved—"

"I know all that." Tristana frowned. "It's just that when I see them together they look so right for each other. She's so marvelous looking, you have to admit it."

"It's what's inside a person that matters."

"Speaking for yourself, Jane?"

"I hope I'm kinder than she is even if I'd win no beauty prizes."

"It isn't compassion that men want, it's passion, and from what I hear...."

"Yes, what do you hear?" Janie tensed, for she guessed what was coming.

"Pagan sleeps in his own bed from all accounts. Isn't it a little too soon for him to have lost interest in that sort of thing?"

"Isn't it bad manners, Tristana, to discuss your

brother's sleeping habits with the maids? I bet it's something you didn't dream of doing before Roxanne came back on the scene. Is that what you are, her spy who digs up bones for her to chew on?"

Tristana flushed deeply.

"Watch yourself, Tris," Janie said quietly. "You're allowing a serpent to whisper in your ear, but she won't thank you for doing her dirty work. Can't you see it?"

"I don't see Pagan looking like a man who's head over heels in love," Tristana rejoined. "Sometimes he looks as moody as the devil, as if he has some awful worry on his mind. I think he's realized that he's made a big mistake where you're concerned.... So what are you going to do about it, Jane?"

Janie had no ready answer to a question that hurt so much. She knew only too well that Pagan was keeping his distance. He rarely came into her room so that almost like strangers they only met at mealtimes. He was always polite, even kind at times, but Janie wanted far more than that from him.

He was her husband and she wanted him to want her. Sometimes at night she contemplated going into his room, but always she was haunted by his rejection of her.

There was a jingle of teacups on a trolley and Tristana followed it into the afternoon room. The thought of tea was inviting but Janie had had enough of sparring with Pagan's sister. They might have been friends.... Everything might have worked out if Roxanne hadn't returned to spoil Pagan's life all over again.

It was a pity, Janie thought as she ran upstairs, that Roxanne hadn't broken her neck instead of wrenching her ankle.

CHAPTER TEN

WITH ROXANNE actually in the house it was difficult for Janie to push her out of mind. She had the housemaids as well as her own maid Celeste waiting on her hand and ankle. Trays of snacks whenever she felt inclined, massages and manicures, a television in her room, long telephone calls to friends not only in London but as far afield as Cap Ferrat. It seemed not to bother her at all that the staff had jobs of their own to attend to, and that long-distance phone calls cost money.

She was, Janie thought fiercely, treating the Towers like a hotel whose management had said it was an honor to have her and she needn't bother about paying any bills.

What was even more infuriating for Janie was Pagan's attitude. He was allowing the house to be disrupted and was leaving it to Janie to settle any arguments that arose in the kitchen when bells started ringing and demands for cups of coffee were issued to out-of-breath maids who had dashed up in answer to the bell from the patient's bedroom.

If Janie had suspected that Roxanne was a spoiled beauty, she now had the evidence right under her nose. If she also suspected that Roxanne's injury was less debilitating than she made out, there seemed little Janie could do about it when the doctor himself, fooled by his patient's acting ability, said that she must remain off her ankle for at least a week.

A week that stretched ahead of Janie with all sorts of perils lying in store for her. Roxanne knew her power over men, and Pagan was vulnerable because he had never really got her out of his system. It seemed to Janie more and more that her own marriage to him was like an unrealized dream instead of a reality. And because he left her alone at night, Janie had nothing stable to cling to. He just didn't want her with Roxanne in the house. She felt he had never wanted her except as a means of defiance he now regretted.

Janie didn't dare to think how it would all end.

Then Hunt Lincoln arrived and some of the strain and anxiety was eased for Janie when she found him as attractive and nice as he had sounded over the telephone.

Because he was nice, and because Pagan hadn't snubbed Roxanne but had let her insinuate her way back into his life, Janie was warmer in her reception of Hunt than was possibly wise. She sensed at once that he responded to her, his eyes filled with little lights, like amber wine catching the sunlight. He was tall, lean-cheeked, and she admired the casual, custom-made perfection of his brown suit and beige silk shirt, with smart French cuffs.

He arrived in a veteran Isottal Fraschini car, and he brought with him into the house a large pigskin suitcase smothered in labels that proclaimed him a seasoned traveler.

He looked slowly around him as he stood in the hall, bathed in facets of colored light from the saint windows. "One steps back into time," he said, his American tone of voice striking strange against Janie's ear, which had become accustomed to the Cornishness in Pagan's deep voice. "You seem at home here, Jane. At least you look it. Are you?"

She didn't quite know what to reply but he picked up her answer in her silence.

"Roxanne?" His brows drew together and his glance traveled up the blackwood stairs. "It's a hell of a thing. How could the guy let it happen?"

Janie's hands clenched in the pockets of her cabinboy pants, atop them she wore a sleeveless T-shirt. She looked young, and the old Tudor hall in which she stood with Hunt Lincoln added to her look of vulnerability. Specks of jeweled light danced over her fair hair and her skin, and as his amber gaze came back to her, it was strikingly intent. He was, she realized, a little like Pagan to look at. An elusive likeness and yet it was there.... He must have caught the curiosity in her gaze for he said, with a slight laugh, "Pagan and I are related from way, way back. I'm rather on the wrong side of the blanket. A Pentrevah girl got herself in trouble with a young trawlerman and they eloped to the States. Unfortunately the young man got into a brawl and was knifed before they reached America. She was a young woman of spirit and she had her baby and somehow survived until she made a remarkably good marriage with a scion of the Lincoln family of Long Island—no relation to the great man, let me add."

"You're an artist, aren't you?" she smiled. "In a way that makes us kindred spirits because I'm an actress.... At least I was before I married Pagan."

"Interesting," Hunt murmured. "Is he going to allow you to continue with your career?"

"We haven't discussed it."

"Do you feel that you'd like to?"

"In a way," she admitted. "But it would hardly be practical because Pagan's life is here and I don't think he'd care for divided loyalties. I was quite certain that

I was going to spend my life in the theater. I still have
moments when I can't quite believe that I've given it
up in order to be a wife."

"I didn't quite know how to picture you, Jane, until
I spoke to you over the phone. You do match your
voice. You're charming."

"Thank you." Janie knew he wasn't flirting with
her but his compliment held an underlying warmth
she couldn't help but feel. It seemed to steal into her
body and ease a little the aching apprehension she had
been feeling these past few days.

The weather had been unreliable and right now the
westering sun sulked through the windows in a glower
of dusky gold and red. As the hall clock chimed Janie
remembered to be a hostess. "Pagan had to go and
see one of his tenants," she said. "You must be longing for some tea, or do you want to go up to your
room first, Mr. Lincoln?"

"The name is Hunt." His lip quirked, as if it
slightly amused him that she was mistress of this rambling *plas* with its towers and its Tudor paneling, and
its traditions that she must accept and become part of.
And in time like other Pentrevah wives be painted
and hung in a frame upon one of the walls as evidence
that she had lived here...and loved here.

"If Mrs. Pelham has made one of her peach-and-
apple pies for tea, then lead me to it, Jane."

She led him into the afternoon room where a log
fire was burning and the two dogs were stretched out
on the great shaggy carpet in front of the fireplace.
They stirred just long enough to size up the visitor,
then flopped back lazily, great heads resting upon
their lionlike paws.

Hunt glanced around him and with a quiet sigh of
pleasure sat down on the great wagon-seat sofa.

"There's nothing in the world like an English country house." He looked around him at the mullioned bookcases, at chairs black as spiders and intricately carved, at the curio cabinets stocked with bric-a-brac collected through the years by the various wives and daughters of the Pentrevah men. His keen amber-shaded eyes took in the paintings on the paneled walls, and then his gaze returned to Janie and he watched as she poured tea from the silver pot.

"Do you take cream and sugar, Mr.—Hunt?"

"Both, please. If I'm going to collect a paunch now I'm approaching middle-age, then I'll do it good-naturedly. I never did favor self-denial, which is why I'm glad Pagan has married again. I wish he'd let me know. I could have been his best man again. I gather it was all very sudden?"

Janie handed him his tea and moved a plate of sandwiches toward him. "Yes," she murmured, and hoped he wouldn't press for details. Still they eluded her, lost like stray animals in Prowler's Pool.

"How did Tristana react?"

Janie sipped her tea. "How you would expect? She's very Cornish and regards me as an outsider. I haven't the dramatic appeal of Roxanne—my compassion is a watered-down version of the passion he had with her and, according to Tris, still wants."

"What does he want according to you, Jane?"

She gave a slight shrug and placed a couple of salmon sandwiches on her plate. "Roxanne is here in the house so that probably answers your question."

"He may have felt obliged to offer hospitality as she had the accident on his land. Pagan is very aware of his obligations as Pentrevah, so don't jump to conclusions that could hurt your marriage, Jane. You have private access to him. You know what I'm getting at?"

"Yes." She took a halfhearted bite out of a sand-wich.

"It's in the private area that you'd notice a change in him, but I don't imagine you have."

"I have!"

She felt his reaction instantly, the stillness in him as he gazed intently at her.

"You aren't telling me—"

"Pagan has lost interest in me." She felt a stab of pain at being disloyal to him. But it hurt even more that he had let Roxanne into the house when he had sworn that he wanted to be rid of her; when he had actually pleaded with Janie not to say that Roxanne was in his heart for always.

"I'm sure that can't be true, Jane."

"I should know." She picked up the teapot and tried to hold it steady as she poured more tea into their cups. Some of the tea slopped into the saucers and she said sorry in the husky voice of someone not far from tears.

"And I should have known better and not married him," she added. "He told me about Roxanne—he didn't try to hide anything—but he kept on saying he needed me and I-I fell for it. I should have kept on going and I shouldn't have looked back, now my life's all upside down. It isn't fair, not when I had every-thing all planned out. I was going to have a career and nothing, no one was going to interfere with it. I was going to make a success of being an actress.... I cer-tainly haven't made a success of being a wife!"

"You poor kid!" Hunt said it softly and sincerely in his American drawl. "You are in a pickle, aren't you? You love him a lot?"

She thought about it. "If love hurts, then I love him," she agreed.

"Then for heaven's sake put up a fight. Don't let Roxanne take him away from you!"

"Don't you see," she met Hunt's eyes, "I never really had him. All along she's had him, all this time, and I have no way to fight her if he doesn't want me. I have some pride! I'm not going to throw myself at his head and see him look at me as if he wants to push me away. It hurts!"

"Yet he married you, Jane. Why would he do that if what you say is true, it's rather extreme, to marry someone and then only a few weeks later go all cold and distant."

"Pagan thought he could forget Roxanne but it didn't work out that way. As soon as he saw her again I was no longer in the picture. I became the shadow while she took on the substance she always had for him."

Suddenly the deep tormenting pain was too much for Janie and she broke into tears and buried her face in her hands.

"Don't cry so." Hunt put his arms around her. "You'll give yourself a headache and make your nose red. Look, when you cry like this you give in to Roxanne and that's what she's after. She wants to break you down so you can't stand up for yourself. You're Pagan's wife now! You've got the rights she walked out on.... Kid, you weren't here in the old days to see what she did to Pagan. She cut his heart in two, don't you know that? She'll cut his heart right out if she gets him again! Buck yourself up, baby, this is no way to act!"

"I-I can't help it." She sniffled and fumbled for her handkerchief. Hunt drew his own from his pocket and proceeded to wipe her eyes for her.

"It's a shame to spoil those eyes with tears," he

murmured. "They're sealike eyes that change their moods.... I think I'm going to paint you, Jane. Faces and figures are what I do best. Have you seen any of my works? I know Pagan has a couple of my child figures."

She nodded, still a little damp-eyed but recovering. The child portraits mentioned by Hunt were in Pagan's den where he did his bookkeeping and wrote his letters. This man painted faces so alive that the breath could almost be seen on their lips.

"They're beautiful," she said sincerely.

"Thanks." He smiled into her eyes, gray at the moment, the lashes clinging in damp points. "I think I'd like to paint you down in Spanish Bay, with the sea rolling to the sands behind you. Strange, but if I didn't know you were married, I'd find it hard to believe that you'd ever been a wife."

She knew what he meant. Sometimes she caught that look when she faced herself in a mirror, a wide-eyed questioning look, as if she were wondering what it was like in the arms of a lover.

"Why do you want to paint me?" she asked. "I'm not a dazzling beauty like Roxanne."

"No, Jane, you're an unaware girl and that is rare."

"Rare?" Her smile was self-mocking. "I'm just an ordinary girl in a rather extraordinary situation."

"Ordinary girls don't get into these sort of situations." He leaned forward as if he felt like kissing her, but she drew back before his lips could touch her.

"Have it your way, Jane, only don't be so unsure of yourself. I believe you're the sort of girl who'd go the stake in support of your beliefs—and your loves."

"A sort of Joan of Arc?" she asked. "I love the Shaw play and would have given anything to star in it."

"Sure you're not burning right now in a fire you've lighted yourself?"

"Meaning?"

"That it's my bet having Roxanne in the house is playing hell with Pagan's libido. Don't condemn him, honey, if you're not altogether sure she's to blame in the sense that he still fancies her."

"I'm unsure of a lot of things," she said with a sigh. "I wander around this house and try to convince myself that it's my home, but all I feel is that I'm a visitor whose staying time is running out."

"Nonsense!" His eyes looked stern. "Roxanne is the visitor and it's her time that's running out."

"She won't leave," Janie exclaimed. "She'd have to be tossed out on her ear and that isn't going to happen, is it? She's had all her belongings brought over from the manor house she's rented. Plum, the girl who maids for me, told me that all her dresses and suits have been hung in the closets of the bedroom she's in and she's making herself well at home."

"Is Pagan aware of what's going on?"

"Naturally!"

"Men aren't always aware of the things that women notice."

"I know, but I don't think anything connected with Roxanne goes unnoticed by Pagan. When he's with me he has such an absent air and I just know he's thinking of her. When I look at him, he avoids my glance. He's sorry he married me!"

Hunt sat looking at her, his face unreadable. Several moments of silence ticked away.

"*If* that's true, Jane, what will you do?"

"Leave him." Her eyes were bleakly gray.

"But you love him. It isn't easy to walk away from love."

"I won't be walking away from it, I shall be taking it with me." She touched her breast. "It's here inside me."

"If it were a child, Jane."

"What are you saying?" Her eyes held a flash of shock.

"You know what I'm saying! If Roxanne has got to him again, she'll do him no good. Fight dirty, Jane!"

"What? Pretend to be...pregnant?"

"Yes. Pagan wants to carry on the Pentrevah tradition by way of a son and that's where he's vulnerable. Do what other women have done in your place, pretend there's a baby on the way, then make sure you flesh out the pretense."

"I couldn't.... Not possibly!"

"You'd sooner see her take him away from you?"

"No!"

"Then what's wrong with a little make-believe if in the long run it's for his own good?"

"Make-believe," she murmured, and a shiver ran through her from the nape of her neck to the base of her spine.

"You've done it on the stage, Jane."

"Yes, but that's different. The audience knows that when the curtain comes down the show is over; we take our bows in front of the curtain and reveal that it's been make-believe. I-I don't think I could deceive Pagan in that way—and I'd be so afraid that he'd guess. He'd never forgive me!"

"Roxanne did worse than that to him," Hunt reminded her.

"He loves Roxanne. He's never stopped loving her. He feels nothing for me, not when he thinks of her, actually in the house, as beautiful as she ever was. I remember saying to him that God gives people a chance to repent, but he said he could never forgive.... Perhaps in some corner of his heart he hasn't forgiven her, but his desire for her is stronger than the hurts, the memories. The longing for her has built up and whatever he felt for me has crumbled away."

"I hate to hear you talk like this, Jane."

"Why should you care?" She gave a shrug. "You hardly know me."

"Some people we know at a glance," he rejoined. "Others we never know because the chemistry is all wrong. We're each other's sort of people and we'd have gotten along had we met in your other world, that of the theater. When I saw you standing out there in the hall I saw your chameleon quality. You're too young to remember but I'm just old enough...there was an actress named Margaret Sullavan and by heck do you remind me of her! Same wide eyes, same air of innocence and nerve, same huskiness in the voice. You couldn't call her a beauty but she had charisma, and you have it, kid, so don't go putting yourself down."

Janie didn't know what to say, but she felt certain he was being sincere, and it felt nice to be told she had charisma, that quality of charm that couldn't be described but was very personal. She remembered when she had played in a repertory production of *The Constant Nymph* the critic on the local newspaper had given her a good write-up and commented on her appealing quality that was spicy-sweet and charming without being cloying.

A log in the fireplace broke apart with a crackle and a flare. Hunt gazed into the flames, then said thoughtfully, "When I look into a fire I think of Roxanne. I saw the witch fire in her eyes the evening of her marriage to Pagan. I saw what she was behind all that physical beauty, but it was too late for Pagan, he'd married her for better or worse, and sadly for him it was for the worse. Jane, you're different. Hang in there, kid, for his sake!''

"What about mine?" she murmured.

"Forsaking all others, Jane."

"Yes," she agreed, "except that I can't remember saying the words."

She went on to explain about her accident in the parking lot. Hunt looked at her searchingly, then forked peach-and-apple pie into his mouth. "This is great! So you had an argument, so what? Married folks have fights so they can enjoy a truce. You say you had concussion?"

"Only slight but it left me with a few mental blanks. One of them being that I can't remember what I wore at my wedding, nor what I said, though I imagine I made the correct responses. It will all come back with a rush but in the meantime it's unsettling."

"It must be. I'm going to make a hog of myself and have another piece of this peachy pie. Join me, eh?"

"I...all right." It had helped talking to Hunt, but nothing had really been solved. How could she really describe what she felt when Pagan gave her that distant look, then dismissed her with a polite good-night and walked into his room, closing behind him a door that felt to her like a hundred-foot wall with spikes along the tip of it.

If only—her heartbeats quickened—if only she had the nerve to make out to him that she was having a baby. He'd want her then; he was that kind of a man. He wouldn't let Roxanne come before his child.... Oh, God, how marvelous to be able to give him what Roxanne had taken away from him!

"That was a deep, deep sigh," Hunt broke in on her thoughts.

She gave him a fleeting smile. "This is good pie."

"That wasn't what you were thinking, was it?"

She shook her head. "Hunt, I don't feel betrayed. That can only happen if someone says they love you. Pagan's never said it to me.... I wouldn't forget something like that."

"So you're going to let your marriage break up, is that it?"

"I think it's broken already."

"Can't it be mended?"

"Not in the way you suggested. I—I wish I could do it—"

"Do it, Jane," Hunt said softly. "The role doesn't call for a lot of dialogue and if you blush like mad it can only help."

"Hunt, you're encouraging me to be wicked."

"You couldn't be wicked if the Devil himself gave you the key to his box of sins. Honey, you wouldn't be the first girl to get her man that way. Isn't he worth a baby lie?"

She caught her breath as she thought of Pagan, big and dark, his hands roughened from riding on her skin, melting her even as he froze himself and turned away from her.

"Yes! Oh, yes!"

"Then do it!"

"Dare I?" She saw the scene shaping itself in her mind, heard herself saying the words, felt his arms crushing her close to him.

"You dared to marry him, honey."

So I did, she thought. *I'm Pagan's wife, not that woman upstairs with her foot on a cushion, lolling against pillows with her skin-tone nightdress plunging down to re-*

*veal her breasts, the musky scent of ambergris in a cloud
around her, the flame hair in brazen disarray.*

The distaste welled up in Janie until she felt she'd
choke on it. Yes, she owed it to herself to put up a
fight. She loved Pagan for himself and wasn't out to
enslave him with her body. Admittedly she was no
match for Roxanne when it came to curves and experience, but as Hunt intimated there was nothing to
stop her from using underhand tactics.

Janie's hands crept together in her lap and her
fingers clung to each other. Had she the nerve to be
so outrageous as to tell Pagan that she had his child
inside her?

Tiny nerves clenched inside her. She felt tremors of
terror and expectation, for if she convinced him she
was carrying, she would then have to ensure that her
lie became a truth.

"Hunt!"

Pagan had stepped into the room and then been
brought to a halt by the astonishment of seeing his
best friend. "I took that darned suitcase out there in
the hall to be another of Roxanne's." His voice
tapered there as if it suddenly hit him that Hunt, as
well as other people, were going to think it strange if
not significant that he had his former wife staying
under the same roof as his present one.

Janie tingled at guilty thoughts at seeing Pagan,
black hair ruffled from his gallop across the moors,
his knee-high boots and well-worn breeches aiding his
look of power and bringing into focus the fact that
Hunt Lincoln was a sophisticated man with a casual
elegance about him. There was an elusive likeness between the two men but Janie knew that where emotions were concerned they were unalike. Pagan was
governed by passions deeper than Hunt's, and at the

same time he was more able to control them. A great love stirred Janie's heart. She knew in that moment that she'd have given her soul to be loved by Pagan, and there was pain and fury in knowing that Roxanne was after him again.

I'll kill her first! And Janie resolved then and there to take Hunt's advice. She'd lie her head off sooner than see that woman back in Pagan's heart and house.

He's mine, Janie told herself. *Mine!*

She caught Pagan's glance and had no idea that her eyes were pure emerald in that fleeting clash of looks, and that her face in contrast was white with emotion.

"Hunt, how good to see you again." The two men shook hands while Janie rang for the maid to bring some fresh hot coffee. Pagan sprawled into an armchair and brushed a hand over his hair.

"I had to go and settle an interesting dispute," he smiled. "You know old Ben Lazarus, who has that stone farmhouse of mine at Flute Tor, a tenancy from way back? Well, it seems he's been putting out water for his dogs in a china bowl that caught the vicar's eye when he came collecting for a jumble sale. He offered old Ben a pound for the bowl and Ben let him have it for the sale, then it turned out that the vicar gave the bowl a good wash and took it to be valued by a local dealer in antiques. The bowl turns out to be a genuine article of Cornish stoneware, a bit worn and cracked in one or two places but nevertheless still worth a considerable bit of money. Right away Ben demanded that the bowl be returned to him, but the vicar wasn't having that as he rightly said he had bought the bowl and paid Ben for it, thinking at the time he wasn't likely to get more than a couple of pounds at the sale.

"Well, old Ben appealed to me to arbitrate and I agreed. The upshot is that he and the vicar are to share the proceeds when the bowl is bid for not at the jumble sale but at a real auction. The vicar's half will go toward his restoration fund, while Ben, would you believe it, has decided to go out to New Zealand to visit his daughter who went out there as a nanny and stayed to marry her boss."

A smile creased Pagan's face. "I've quite enjoyed my afternoon. It isn't often that a dog's water bowl turns out to be a close cousin to a Ming dish."

The coffee arrived, the two men fell to talking, and Janie slipped away to her room. She needed to make a plan of action, and to get up the nerve to carry it out.

Her resolve was strengthened when she passed the big guest room and through the partly open door heard Roxanne taking her maid to task in a voice that was the epitome of edged insolence.

"You fool of a girl, you don't wash crepe de chine in hot water, it has to be lukewarm. Just look what you've done to the slip—unless you hoped I'd give it to you if it shrunk!"

These words were followed by a ripping sound and Janie guessed that Roxanne was destroying the silk garment rather than give it away. Janie stood hesitant on the gallery. She had never used the word before, but suddenly she wanted to rush into the room and tell Roxanne that she was a bitch, and she'd better pack her cases right away and clear out of the Towers.

"Now get out," Roxanne said to her maid. "I'm going to have an hour's nap. Wake me about six-thirty for my bath. I'm going downstairs this evening and I'll wear my ivory satin with the black pearls."

"Y-you can't walk down on that ankle, madam."

"I intend to be carried down in a pair of strong arms. I was married to the owner of them and he carried me upstairs more than once!"

The implication was obvious and Janie fled to get away from it. There was to be no escape from what she must do if she was to save Pagan from being caught on Roxanne's baited hook.

CHAPTER ELEVEN

THE DRESS was of chiffon, lovely and flowing as shadows trapped in green sea. Her hair shone and her skin and lips were lightly made up. On her feet were silver-kid evening shoes with slender heels.

Janie had made herself as glamorous as possible, and now she stood by a window on the gallery, gathering her composure for the descent to the drawing room. The window was slightly open and she breathed the night air from off the moors into which a dash of the sea had been distilled. Above the towers and gables of the house floated the filmy arc of a new moon, and Janie made a wish and begged the moon witch to grant it.

She was so faraway in her thoughts that she gave a visible jump when a hand touched her arm. She turned and Pagan was standing there, tall and always impressive in dark evening wear. She stood very still, quite unable to smile as his eyes swept her up and down.

"You look rather special," he murmured. "I haven't seen that dress before. It isn't one I bought you, is it?"

She shook her head. "It's my own party dress. Do you like it?"

"It's very pleasing on you, Jane."

"Thank you."

"Is it in honor of Hunt? I noticed you were getting

on well with him, but most women seem to. He courts them all but marries none of them.''

"Perhaps that makes him wise.''

"You consider marriage unwise?''

"Don't you?'' Even in heeled shoes she had to look up at him and his eyes were shadowed gold, his features stern and distinctive, so that as she looked at him she felt a barrier between them that was becoming progressively harder to cross. It wasn't right for it to be there, not between two people who were man and wife. She wanted him to put his arms around her and crush her in her chiffon to his hard warm body. But he didn't make the slightest move to touch and she knew why; he wanted a barrier between them because the one between him and Roxanne was falling down.

"Sir!''

Pagan turned and Roxanne's maid was standing there.

"Madam wants to dine with the family, sir, and she asks will you carry her downstairs?''

Janie glanced at him to catch his reaction but if he was eager to do Roxanne's bidding it didn't show on his face.

"Very well,'' he said politely. "I'll be along in a moment.''

The maid hastened away and when he looked at Janie he merely said, "You go on down to the drawing room and have a drink. I'm sure Hunt will be delighted to amuse you.''

"Just as Roxanne will be delighted to amuse you?'' Janie couldn't stop herself from asking.

"She's a guest in this house,'' he said impassively. "The Pentrevahs do their best to respect the wishes of a guest.''

"I'm sure you'll do your utmost." Janie's voice shook, in fact the tremulous feeling seemed to attack her all over.

Abruptly Pagan leaned toward her and his nostrils tensed. "Don't drive me to the edge, Jane, my control isn't that absolute."

"What edge are you talking about?"

"Don't you know?" His eyes raked hers.

Janie's heart sank. Yes, she knew that he was teetering on the edge of falling as hard for Roxanne as he had fallen long ago, long before Janie met him one dark night on the moor.

"You'd better not keep her waiting." Janie tried to step past him so she could go downstairs, but still he loomed above her and she felt the threat that emanated from him, seething in his blood and sinews. Something clamored in her blood. *Now*, cried a voice in her head. *Do it . . . say it now.*

"And while I'm at it," her heart was clamoring, "I'd better tell you that I'm going to have a baby."

His silence was a thunder that shook Janie from head to toe, then frantically she was pushing past him and she took the stairs in such flight that she reached the hall as if she actually flew down them. She half ran toward the double doors of the drawing room, not daring to look back but sensing that he still stood thunderstruck up there on the gallery where she had left him.

She hadn't planned to come out with it like that. Her plan in fact had revolved around a bedroom scene, soft lights, the stage set for her to find herself in his arms, halfway to making her fabrication become a fact.

Janie entered the drawing room to the click of mahjongg ivory pieces on the gamestable where Tristana and Hunt played together. She returned Hunt's smile and let her shaking knees sink her into a chair. It was done, she had dropped her bombshell on Roxanne's high hopes and now it rested with Pagan to see if the sexual pull of a woman was stronger than his urge to hold in his arms the Pentrevah heir.

"Pour yourself a sherry," Tristana urged. "Hunt tells me it was he who had you on the phone. Why didn't you say?"

"I wanted to surprise you.... You'd better move that castle of yours or I shall move in and take over."

"You may move in on me any time you like, Hunt."

"Don't tempt me, honey, especially tonight when you're wearing a dress instead of a pair of breeches scented with stable. What's all the glamour in aid of— or do I guess?"

"As you know women so well, Hunt, your guess is bound to be spot on."

"The divinity is dining with us and the pair of you feel the urge to compete, is that it?"

"Is that it, Jane?" Tristana turned in her chair to stare across the room at Janie; a high, wide, gracefully proportioned room, whose shaded lamps cast tinted shadows over the patina of old fine furniture, the glimmer of gold leaf in picture frames, the prisms of decanters and wineglasses standing upon silver. At the windows hung silvery brocade, across the floor stretched an oriental carpet like a peacock's tail, a grand piano stood black and shiny in an alcove.

"My word, Jane, you have made an effort."

There were flushes across Janie's cheekbones and she felt feverish, and riddled with guilt.

"Oh, this old thing." She flicked at her skirt and didn't notice that a chiffon panel flew perilously close to the fire in the great hearth. "I've had it for ages."

"The color suits you," Hunt drawled. He rose to his feet and approached the liquor cabinet. "You'll have a sherry, Jane?"

"Please."

There was a musical clink as he drew the stopper from the sherry decanter; the deep gold liquid looked inviting in the stemmed glasses.

"Bonheur!" Hunt raised his glass. "The company of two attractive girls is my idea of happiness."

"Wouldn't the sole company of a single girl be even more inviting?" Tristana said seductively. She wore a black dress with lacy sleeves and had taken the trouble to groom her thick dark hair and place a Spanish comb in it. If there was Spanish blood in the Pentrevahs then it certainly showed in Tristana, thought Janie. She also had a feeling that Pagan's sister was attracted to Hunt but not quite certain what to do about it. He had been Pagan's friend for so long that she didn't know whether to regard him as a brother, that was Janie's feeling.

Janie sympathized with her if she was in a bit of a turmoil where her emotions were concerned. Tristana could handle any kind of a horse, no matter how high tempered, but a man was far more complex. Hunt Lincoln might regard her as a sister.

"Or do you think there's safety in numbers?" Tristana pursued.

He smiled and studied the firelight in his sherry. "Most men, Tris, are rather like hummingbirds and they'll take nourishment from every flower that will let them. Of course, when a hummingbird gets attracted to one particular bloom, then he'll go into a crazy spin and may want to stay that way, no longer able to find pleasure in flitting from one flower to another. Having zoomed in on what takes his fancy, then the rose in the next bed, or the honeysuckle sprawled upon a wall, or a violet laid out under a shady tree, might as well not be there for all the notice he takes. Nature is strange and awesome, is it not?''

Tristana gazed at him with fascinated dark eyes. "If you hadn't become a painter, Hunt, you could have been a writer," she said admiringly.

His amber eyes kindled into a smile. "I wouldn't be much of a success as a writer in this day and age, my dear. The symbolic language of romance is now a dying art and even Byron would have found it difficult to make a living. Once upon a time the word love had meaning, but these days love has become the X ingredient in sex.''

Janie flinched. Was it true that sex was more important to people these days than love? She knew the look of Pagan made her heart beat fast, but she also felt a yearning to care for him and guard him from getting hurt.

"Don't say that about love!" she exclaimed. "What would anything be worth if we didn't have it to look forward to? I-I used to think it might be only a word in a song, only a line men spun to hook a girl, but I no longer feel that way. It does exist! You can actually feel it when you touch someone you love!''

"You're right, Jane." Hunt said it decisively. "It's the creative and destructive force in all of us. It can glow like that diamond on your hand, or it can wear a dark mask and slash the soul out of us. What's happening these days is that people are becoming wary of giving themselves. They only give their bodies and keep their souls in some kind of personal freezer. It sure could kill love and that would be a pity.''

"Hunt, you're making me shiver!" Tristana exclaimed.

Janie sat and gazed at the ring on her left hand. It

was a celestial diamond alive with tiny fires and it had to mean something.... She strove to break through the mental block that prevented her from remembering what she had felt on her wedding day and whether there had been a beckoning warmth in Pagan's eyes instead of a distant coolness.

What had it been like on their wedding night? Had there been tenderness and then a passion that swept her mind out of her body so there was nothing but Pagan's possession...nobody but him in all her world?

Even as she sought the vital answer to her question Pagan strode into the drawing room carrying Roxanne in his arms. It was a vivid and instant picture that knifed through Janie, the curvaceous arms around his neck, the flame head against his shoulders, her eyes holding a brazen sensuousness in the frame of long lashes.

"Darlings!" Her voice throbbed. "Look at me, aren't I brave? I just couldn't stand being alone while a party is going on down here. Isn't Pagan strong, but then you always were, weren't you, darling?"

He strode with her to a big velvet couch and as he lowered her to it, her arms still clung around him and her eyes seemed to be devouring him. She had such an air of insolent, languorous self-satisfaction that Janie could hardly bear it. She saw the tip of Roxanne's tongue run its moistness around her red lips. She looked as sinful and erotic as a Rubens painting.

"Hello, Hunt." She sank back against the velvet as Pagan straightened his tie. Her eyes glinted with wicked green lights. "I am now Roxanne of Ruthvyn Manor. Sounds fearfully grand, doesn't it?"

"I've been told that you're now a merry widow," Hunt rejoined.

"Yes, I'm quite well-off and it's nice." Her tinted

fingers played with the black pearls that hung against her bare skin. Her ivory satin dress was sleeveless and cut very low. Janie looked at Pagan who had his back to her and seemed to be ignoring her.

"How did he die?" Hunt handed her a sherry. "Did you give him a Borgia cocktail?"

"Hunt, really!" She laughed and sipped her sherry. "He died of natural causes."

"Worn out, honey?"

"You could say so. He worked so hard, poor dear, on all those corporations."

Her gaze slid to Pagan and went up and down his tall frame. Janie could stand no more. She had to get out of this room, out of the scent and sight of that woman who had about her the silky indolence of a sea anemone in the process of digesting a victim.

Janie jumped to her feet and even as she did so a greedy flame licked out of the fire and caught light to the chiffon panel of her dress that had wafted too close when she had first sat down. As the flame leaped to engulf her there came a scream—but not from Janie. It came from Tristana and it alerted Pagan.

"My God! Look out, Jane!"

He looked, he leaped and at the same time dragged from the piano a heavy silk shawl that lay over it. He whipped it at Janie, literally beat at her with it until the chiffon no longer flared and lay in tangled ribbons around her sobbing figure. She was more hurt by the sound whipping he had given her than by the flames. He had acted too speedily for her to have suffered a burn, but she was badly shocked.

"You damn little fool!" Pagan raged. "Why did you have to sit so close to the damn fire?"

"P-perhaps to get warm! All I g-get from you is the

cold s-shoulder! I wish to God I'd never met you let alone m-married you!"

Even as she spoke the word she realized its falsity. Her close brush with danger had released the truth in a blinding flash as alarming as the tongue of flame had been licking at her dress. She rocked on her feet as the truth hit her—she and Pagan had never gone through a marriage service together. It had all been faked in order to fool Roxanne. They weren't husband and wife and she, in her ignorance, had said that to him about a baby.

Janie knew she had gone chalky white. It was as if she had now been flung into a quagmire—a deep and choking pit of humiliation. She wanted to run into a corner and hide from his eyes. As if he would have married her! How could she have thought it let alone believed it!

"Oh, Pagan," Roxanne was actually laughing, as if what she had just witnessed had been comic to her, "wasn't it easier living with a sinner than you're finding it living with a little saint?"

A silence followed her words, heaving to and fro like waves presaging a storm. Then it broke. In a sudden fury Pagan rounded on Roxanne and his voice cracked like doom itself.

"I've had just as much as I can take from you!" His voice was steel, with a cutting edge. "I've had you, Roxie, up to here!" He swiped his forehead with the edge of his hand, where a truant strand of black hair lay caught in the sweat of a savage emotion.

"Get yourself out of my house in the morning and if you value your neck don't ever show yourself to me again! I'll kill you if you do! I'll finish the job once and for all!"

In a kind of daze Janie heard him say these things to Roxanne. The words washed in and out of her mind, and her knees were buckling when Pagan swept her up in his arms, there in front of Roxanne, there in front of his sister and his friend, who had seen Roxanne for what she was all those years ago when Pagan had been blinded by her beauty.

No longer was he blind. He was gazing down at Janie and his eyes were raw gold, brimming with a fire she didn't want him to beat out...ever.

"Do you see this girl?" he shot a look across the room to where Roxanne sat as if turned to ivory. "She's worth a hundred of you, Roxie and I only hope to God I'm worth something to her."

"A nice big house and the rents coming in from your farms," Roxanne said insolently. "I don't imagine she earns much as an actress."

"Go to hell!" Pagan said it with savage insolence, and then he was carrying Janie from the room, across the hall and up the wide sweep of the blackwood stairs.

Janie lay there snugly in his arms and all the pain had ebbed away leaving only pleasure.

Pagan had told Roxanne to go to hell, and he had a look on his face that said he was carrying her up to heaven.

"You're the damned best actress I've met," he drawled. "I nearly jumped out of my skin when you came out with that bit about a baby. What was that all about?"

"I—" she buried her face against his warm throat "—I thought we were married, I really did, and I was scared sick you were going back to—"

"By hell, you couldn't have thought such a thing of me, Jane!" His voice was bruised with pain.

"Y-you acted so cool toward me. You pushed me away from you."

"Yes, because you had this concussed idea that we

were married. Had we really been churched, my girl, no way would I have let you sleep alone in that great big bed. I was running away from myself, nitwit. I wasn't rejecting you!''

Suddenly he groaned and clenched her so tight to him that she gasped.

"How do I say it, how do I make you understand how adorable you are to me? My feelings—they go so much deeper than words. I'm not Hunt, who can use words even as he keeps the key to his heart locked away.''

"Just keep talking, Pagan,'' she begged. "I'll catch on to what you're trying to say. Just say it!''

"When a man is young, Jane, there's no room in his heart for romanticism. All he feels for a woman is passion and once that's satisfied everything else starts to die. Roxanne sledgehammered all my feelings into the ground, and then you came along and the roses started to grow again for me and when I'm close to you I'm drowning in their scent.''

He held her and thrust open a door. The ruby-shaded lamp burned its welcome beside the bed where the sheets were invitingly turned back. Pagan stood her on the rug beside the bed and she smiled with the sweet dazedness of a girl drunk on the wine of love. She felt his fingers at her zipper and the scorched dress fell around her ankles and she kicked it away from her. Her last link with the stage life she had been so certain she wanted.

She gazed up at Pagan and her heart was flooded with her want of him. She could feel the bloom of it spreading over her and there was a radiance in her eyes.

"I love you,'' she said softly, and her body quivered as his hands moved down caressingly to her hips and clasped her to him. They kissed madly, frantically, as if they'd just discovered what love was all about.

Love was two people who couldn't live apart. Love was finding out that loneliness was over and from now on they'd share joy and be together to face the tribulations.

"Love the man and he'll love you in return," Janie's grandmother had wisely said.

"Jane...Jane," he framed her face with his hands and looked deeply into her eyes, "I know you want a career as an actress but I can't share you, do you mind, my darling girl?"

She shook her head. "My stagestruck days are over, Pagan. I don't want you to share me—except perhaps...." A wild pink color washed into her cheeks. "You know what I mean, don't you?"

"I know." His eyes glinted. "We'll call him Dominic, shall we?"

"Or Domini."

"And there'll be laughter in this house again," he said softly. "The laughter of my love."